POTUS

Or, Behind Every Great Dumbass Are Seven Women Trying to Keep Him Alive

by Selina Fillinger

‖SAMUEL FRENCH‖

FOR PRODUCTION INQUIRIES

UNITED STATES AND CANADA
info@concordtheatricals.com
1-866-979-0447

UNITED KINGDOM AND EUROPE
licensing@concordtheatricals.co.uk
020-7054-7298

Each title is subject to availability from Concord Theatricals Corp.,
depending upon country of performance. Please be aware that
POTUS may not be licensed by Concord Theatricals Corp. in your
territory. Professional and amateur producers should contact the
nearest Concord Theatricals Corp. office or licensing partner to verify
availability.

MUSIC AND THIRD-PARTY MATERIALS USE NOTE

IMPORTANT BILLING AND CREDIT REQUIREMENTS

POTUS premiered on Broadway at the Shubert Theatre on April 27, 2022. The production was directed by Susan Stroman, with scenic design by Beowulf Boritt, costume design by Linda Cho, lighting design by Sonoyo Nishikawa, and sound design by Jessica Paz. The production stage manager was Johnny Milani. The cast was as follows:

HARRIET . . . . Julie White

JEAN . . . . Suzy Nakamura

STEPHANIE . . . . Rachel Dratch

DUSTY . . . . Julianne Hough

BERNADETTE . . . . Lea DeLaria

CHRIS . . . . Lilli Cooper

MARGARET . . . . Vanessa Williams

STANDBYS . . . . Gisela Chípe, Anita Abdinezhad,
Jennifer Fouché, Lisa Helmi Johanson

POTUS was originally produced on Broadway by:

Seaview, 51 Entertainment, Glass Half Full, Level Forward

Salman Al-Rashid, Runyonland Productions,
Sony Music Masterworks, One Community

Jay Alix and Una Jackman, Jonathan Demar, Imagine Equal Entertainment,
Lucas Katler, David J. Lynch, Leonid Makaron,
Mark Gordon Pictures, Liz Slager, Ted Snowdon,
Natalie Gorman/Tish Brennan Throop

and the Shubert Organization (Mark Shacket, Executive Producer)

CHARACTERS

In order of their emotional proximity to POTUS (closest to furthest).

HARRIET – His chief of staff.

JEAN – His press secretary.

STEPHANIE – His secretary.

DUSTY – His dalliance.

BERNADETTE – His sister.

CHRIS – A journalist.

MARGARET – His wife. The First Lady.

SETTING

The White House.

Perhaps not the current administration, exactly – but broad strokes of past presidents, combined with stress dreams of future ones.

And, if we're being honest, an amalgamation of them all...

AUTHOR'S NOTES

Note on Text:
An indented and lone semicolon (;) indicates a charged moment of silence. A forward slash (/) indicates where the following line overlaps. Lack of punctuation at the end of a line indicates an interrupted thought.

Note on Set:
Simple, flexible, representative: a few chairs, desks, doors, some ornamental objects, arranged in various configurations to create the sense of endless offices and hallways. Allowing for multiple scenes to occur simultaneously in different parts of the White House.

Rules of the World:
The seven women are the only people onstage, but they frequently address colleagues, press, etc. that we can't see. Those lines should be delivered out, to us. We should have the sense that TVs are everywhere and the news always running – but we only hear soundbites as indicated, when a character clicks into what's being said. We should never see POTUS in his entirety, a leg or two at most.

Note on Casting:
American power structures are rooted in, and shaped by, white supremacy. Racism permeates our institutions, compounding gender and class inequity everywhere, but especially in electoral politics. This play is a critique of complicity in white patriarchy; thus, the following requirements speak to those dynamics and must be followed. International productions should analyze and reflect in their casting a similar understanding of marginalized communities' struggle for voice within their governing bodies.

In America: Bernadette is white. Margaret is Black. Chris is Black. Jean, Harriet, Dusty, and Stephanie can be played by actors of any ethnicity; but be aware that lines and relationships will land differently depending on the racial breakdown of the cast. Some of the insults will be more cringe, some less, depending on the privilege each character possesses. These are interesting dynamics to explore, but they should be interrogated consciously, with care for each community.

At least three of the characters must be women of color. Actors can be cis or trans. Age is flexible. Beauty is subjective. So long as they're fast, fierce, and fucking hilarious.

Note on Music:
When picking the BitchBeats song, think aggressive classic rock or punk rock: Joan Jett, Bikini Kill, Pussy Riot, etc... Please note: A license to produce *POTUS* does not include a performance license for any third-party or copyrighted music.

For any woman who's ever found herself the secondary character in a male farce.

ACT I

1.1

(**HARRIET** *vs.* **JEAN.**)

HARRIET. Cunt.

;

JEAN. What?

HARRIET. Cunt.

JEAN. No.

HARRIET. It's not a question.

JEAN. No.

HARRIET. It's not a yes or no question.

JEAN. Publicly?

HARRIET. Yes.

JEAN. No.

HARRIET. Please stop saying no.

JEAN. How public? Who exactly was there?

HARRIET. *Washington Post.*

JEAN. Well

HARRIET. *Huffington Post.*

JEAN. They're hardly

HARRIET. CNN.

JEAN. Okay

HARRIET. *New York Times*, BBC, and three Chinese diplomats.

JEAN. The ones who speak English?

HARRIET. They all speak English.

JEAN. I think there was one last year who struggled with idioms, you know, like, slang, so it might have gone over / his head

HARRIET. Everyone heard it, everyone got it, two people *gasped*

JEAN. No.

HARRIET. *These are not questions, Jean, stop saying no.*

JEAN. He said the words, "My wife's a cunt?"

     ;

HARRIET. He said, "Please excuse my wife's absence. She's having a cunty morning."

     ;

JEAN. Well that's not so bad

HARRIET. Wow

JEAN. It's not! We can contain that. We all have cunty mornings sometimes. My son has them every week. You're clearly having one today

HARRIET. She was in the room.

JEAN. What?

HARRIET. Margaret wasn't absent, she was in the room. She entered late but she had been there for ten minutes when he

JEAN. Called her absent.

HARRIET. And a cunt.

JEAN. Cunt-y.

HARRIET. If this is you workshopping your response to the press right now

JEAN. I'm just processing, I'm trying to – Why didn't he see her?

HARRIET. She was sitting.

JEAN. And therefore invisible?

HARRIET. He was standing, so the diplomats felt like it would be rude to sit, so they were all standing, they were all standing in front of her, blocking his view and she was sitting.

JEAN. He stood for the entirety of the meeting?

HARRIET. He can't sit right now because of / the thing on his

JEAN. The thing on his – right.

I thought they were removing it.

HARRIET. Well they couldn't remove it last week because of the / shit with Israel

JEAN. Shit with Israel

HARRIET. And there was talk of doing it today but he got booked up: nine a.m. briefing, ten a.m. China, non-proliferation discussions in an hour

JEAN. Okay, but then

HARRIET. Two p.m. Leslie Hopper endorsement

JEAN. Okay, but afterwards

HARRIET. Three p.m. handshakes with the Jacobson twins

JEAN. Can't we reschedule them?

HARRIET. The two veterans who were blinded and maimed while saving their units in Iraq? I'm gonna say no

JEAN. I'm just spit-balling

HARRIET. Three p.m. handshake, five p.m. briefing, six p.m. pedicure

JEAN. Push the pedicure!

HARRIET. Have you *seen* his feet?

JEAN. Okay, blink, Harry, you're not blinking

HARRIET. Pedi, tux, then eight p.m. gala honoring FML!

;

JEAN. What?

HARRIET. FML! FML! The Female Models of Leadership Council.

JEAN. Okay, I think you need to include the Council part in the acronym because – do you know what that means?

HARRIET. I just told you

JEAN. No, but literally

HARRIET. Literally, I've bullied 200 feminists into attending tonight's gala and written thirty-seven drafts of POTUS's speech so that our female base doesn't literally shrink smaller than a nutsack in the snow! It's final hour, we're headed into reelection: FML!

JEAN. But if someone texts you FML it means

HARRIET. The point is he's booked, Jean! He's fucking booked, so they had to reschedule the procedure which is why Margaret entered the meeting late, she was talking to Dr. Rifson and she entered the meeting late and POTUS didn't see her – bing, bang, boom: "cunty."

JEAN. So Margaret agrees with Dr. Rifson that the abscess on his anus should be removed – and that makes her a cunt?

HARRIET. He's pissed she's insisting on surgery. His friend, Jerry, from college said that he had the same thing and that it just went away without surgery.

JEAN. What the fuck does Jerry know?

HARRIET. He said he should rub tea tree oil on it

JEAN. How does a person even get an anal abscess?

HARRIET. Jerry told him it can happen sometimes from ass play.

;

Ass play.

When it's rough.

Ass play

JEAN. I know / what ass play is

HARRIET. When it's rough ass play.

JEAN. *Stop saying ass play.*

;

Is that particular activity a plausible cause for *this* anal abscess?

HARRIET. How would I know?

JEAN. You're his right-hand.

HARRIET. Not for *that* activity.

JEAN. You're his chief of staff.

HARRIET. Exactly. You want to know about stuff like that, ask the First Lady.

JEAN. Right, like Margaret would ever go anywhere / near his

HARRIET. She would know if he was engaging in that kind of thing with anyone else

JEAN. Why would she know that?

HARRIET. Because it's HIM and it's HER and it's their weird marriage with all their weird "arrangements"!

JEAN. Well she and I don't have an "arrangement," so I can't just go up to the First Lady and ask if her husband is getting into rough ass play with some other

HARRIET. I'm just saying if you want to know

JEAN. WANT to know? I don't WANT to know. In the last three years, I've had to bail on seven first dates and my sister's mastectomy just to spin shit I don't WANT TO KNOW.

And right now I'm trying to figure out if my biggest problem today will be explaining why the President of the United States used the word "cunty" to describe his wife to three diplomats – OR if there is still something MORE awful involving ASS PLAY that I need to know about!

IS there, Harriet? Is this day about to become an oozing pustule on the anus of my week?

Or is everything *fine*?

1.2

*(MARGARET vs. STEPHANIE. STEPHANIE
has flung herself in front of the closed door,
blocking MARGARET's path. MARGARET,
seething, wears an impeccable suit and Crocs.)*

STEPHANIE. No!

MARGARET. I'm gonna punt that man's abscessed ass across the South Lawn and if you don't get out of my way I will shred you like the sad cardigan you are.

STEPHANIE. Ma'am, he really is busy

MARGARET. With what.

STEPHANIE. You know that I can't

MARGARET. If he's in there rubbing tea tree oil on his

STEPHANIE. He is not, Ma'am. Anymore. But he is in the middle of

MARGARET. I checked his schedule and I know he has a break right now.

STEPHANIE. Something came up.

MARGARET. Did it?

STEPHANIE. Yes, Ma'am.

MARGARET. Margaret.

STEPHANIE. Pardon?

MARGARET. Margaret or Margie. Do not address me as Ma'am. I sent a memo this morning.

STEPHANIE. Yes, Ma'am – Margaret – Margie – Why are we calling you by your name now?

MARGARET. To show how earthy I am.

STEPHANIE. Okay

MARGARET. *(Bitterly.)* Because apparently these days it's not enough to be wildly accomplished and deeply effective

STEPHANIE. Ohh is this about the

MARGARET. I've launched free lunch programs in 6,000 public schools but all Twitter can twat about are the stilettos I wore to *one* homeless shelter

STEPHANIE. Is that why you're wearing

MARGARET. *(Scathingly.)* What do *you* think, Stephanie? You think this was *my* idea? You think when I gave my speech as Valedictorian I said, "One day I will walk the halls of the White House in shoes that can double as flotation devices"? No! But there are children to feed, funds to raise, and *Time Magazine* is interviewing me today for their Women of Excellence series so I will not allow anything to distract from my work – *(Going for the door again.)* – least of all

STEPHANIE. Ma'am – Margaret – Margie – I am the Presidential Secretary and nobody enters that door without my say-so!

> *(She hits a wide stance, arms above her head in a V, hands clenched into fists.)*

MARGARET. What's happening?

STEPHANIE. Harriet gave me a book about women taking up space in the workplace and I've read it twice!

MARGARET. Are you having a stroke?

STEPHANIE. I'm power-stancing, I am decreasing my cortisol levels and increasing my testosterone, thus increasing my confidence!

> (**HARRIET** *opens the door, hitting* **STEPHANIE** *hard in the back and knocking her over.)*

OW!

HARRIET. Jesus. Stephanie, what the hell are you doing? *(To* **MARGARET.**) What's on your feet?

MARGARET. Does *anyone* read my memos?

STEPHANIE. *(Frantically, to* **HARRIET.**) She wanted to see the president and I said no! My spine was in alignment and I used declarative sentences!

HARRIET. *(Soothing.)* That's great – Have you been listening to that playlist I recommended?

STEPHANIE. BitchBeats, yes Ma'am, very empowering, I listen to it every morning while I eat my overnight oats.

HARRIET. Why don't you go practice your power stances in the bathroom.

> *(***STEPHANIE** *scurries to the door, then turns back to say something.)*

MARGARET. *That* trash fire *must* be extinguished.

HARRIET. She's still in the room, Margaret – Yes, Stephanie?

STEPHANIE. *(A whimper.)* The merch for the Female Models of Leadership Council arrived.

HARRIET. Thank you.

> *(***STEPHANIE** *flees.)*

MARGARET. She's like a menopausal toddler.

HARRIET. Stephanie has a photographic memory and speaks five languages. To what do I owe the pleasure, Margaret?

MARGARET. I actually need a chat with POTUS, so if you'll just / excuse me

HARRIET. *(Blocking the door.)* He didn't mean it. He's in a lot of pain and it's clouding his judgment.

MARGARET. Your loyalty to my husband is admirable, and I hope you continue to feel fulfilled by your choice to trade youth and beauty for a life of service to him.

HARRIET. *(Darkly.)* Thank you

MARGARET. But if you do not let me speak to POTUS right now, I refuse to attend the Female Models of Leadership dinner this evening.

HARRIET. We both know that would hit your ratings harder than his.

MARGARET. Dammit, Harriet, you cannot prevent me from having a marital discussion with my husband!

HARRIET. I absolutely can, on any day during his term in office, but especially today, when he has a nuclear non-proliferation meeting in half an hour, a gubernatorial candidate endorsement in two, and an oozing pustule on his anus. I finally got him calmed down from your argument this morning

MARGARET. What argument? / It wasn't an argument

HARRIET. When you told him to stop behaving like his father, grow a pair, and have the procedure without anesthesia.

MARGARET. I had two natural births and one root canal with no drugs, he can certainly

HARRIET. He's not in his right mind and he's making terrible decisions

MARGARET. What else is new

HARRIET. *(Low.)* He wants to pardon Bernadette

MARGARET. He wants to PARDON / BERNADETTE?

HARRIET. Lower your voice! He had a phone call with her yesterday and you know how manipulative she can be, especially when he's feeling vulnerable

MARGARET. We've talked about this! You can't pardon someone just because she's your baby sister!

HARRIET. I know.

MARGARET. Our ratings would plummet! We would be crucified! She's wanted in three countries, Harry

HARRIET. *I know.*

MARGARET. Not to mention all the holidays we'd have to start spending with her if she were to get out – You know, Bernadette bought my daughter a dildo for her sixteenth birthday? And stole my ruby earrings, probably wears them as nipple piercings now

HARRIET. I KNOW I FUCKING KNOW, which is why we're not going to let him go through with it, but if you don't back off and let me handle this

JEAN. I'm sorry, did someone say something about Bernadette?

(**JEAN** *stands in the doorway.*)

HARRIET. Nope / don't think so, nobody said that

MARGARET. Of course not, nothing to worry about.

JEAN. Okay 'cause I'm going into the press room right now and if there's something I need to know

HARRIET.	**MARGARET.**
You don't need to know anything, Jean.	Nothing to know. Everything's fine.

(Pumping herself up, heading to the press room:)

JEAN. *(Cracking her neck.)* Okay let's go, fuck me

HARRIET.	**MARGARET.**
(With weak cheer.) Go get 'em! Wooohh	*(With weak cheer.)* You got this! Knock 'em dead

JEAN. *(Exiting irritably.)* Oh shut up

1.3

(CHRIS vs. JEAN. CHRIS sits at Jean's desk, hooked up to a breast pump.)

CHRIS. Hi!

JEAN. Leave.

CHRIS. *(Cheerfully.)* And a cunty morning to you! What a time to be alive, isn't it?

JEAN. God, that thing is loud. You can't pump in my office.

CHRIS. Where else am I gonna do it in this hellish place?

JEAN. Not my problem. Put 'em away. How did you get back here before me?

CHRIS. I know a shortcut from the press room. I thought you handled it very well in there.

JEAN. You have food on your collar.

CHRIS. The twins just discovered projectile vomiting.

JEAN. I have an extra shirt you can borrow.

CHRIS. As much as I love your Steve Jobs aesthetic

JEAN. *(Loftily.)* Turtlenecks are universally flattering.

CHRIS. I'll stick with the vomit. How would you say your morning's going, on a spectrum of cocky to cunty?

JEAN. Do you have something for me, or are you just craving companionship since Greg left you?

CHRIS. Bahrain.

JEAN. What about it.

CHRIS. It's a country

JEAN. I know.

CHRIS. Involved in the nuclear non-proliferation discussions

JEAN. I'm aware.

CHRIS. Occurring in fifteen minutes

JEAN. *Get there.*

CHRIS. Bahrain is pissy about cunty.

JEAN. How do you know?

CHRIS. I've got a buddy at HuffPo who covers the area. The prime minister's unsettled by the fact that the president would be so blatantly disrespectful to someone so close to him.

JEAN. I don't think a government as cozy with Saudi Arabia as *Bahrain's* can really pass judgment on ours.

CHRIS. I don't think a government as cozy with Saudi Arabia as ours can really pass judgment on *Bahrain.*

JEAN. We're in bed with their oil, not their gender politics.

CHRIS. *(Enjoying herself.)* Is that your official comment?

JEAN. No.

CHRIS. Was it an *emphasized* cunty? Or more of a casual, throw-away / cunty?

JEAN. *What do you want, Chris?*

CHRIS. A comment.

JEAN. You got my comment in the press room.

CHRIS. I want a better one.

JEAN. I thought you said I handled it well.

CHRIS. *(Enjoying herself.)* Yeah, so handle it poorly for me and I'll make it anonymous.

JEAN. Very cute.

CHRIS. Speaking of fucking adorable, can you please tell Luke to stop sharing his snacks with Kenny? We're trying to get him out of the habit of sharing food at school because of his canola allergy.

JEAN. I'm not going to tell my kid to be less generous because your kid has trouble saying no. I'm raising a feminist.

CHRIS. Yeah, foisting his agenda onto someone who is too polite to refuse sounds super feminist.

JEAN. *Sharing* is not *foisting*, *grapes* are not an *agenda*, and you're *not supposed to be here*

CHRIS. I'm a White House reporter.

JEAN. Doing a fluff piece on the First Lady's excellence for *Time*. Sounds like someone's being phased out. Who are they replacing you with? Young Harvey? Younger Nate? That giggly boy from BuzzFeed?

CHRIS. Listen

JEAN. No, *you* listen: You are a newly divorced mother of three with vomit on your neck and tit juice on your shirt. These guys can out-tweet you, out-text you, chug a Red Bull and work three days straight. Is it fair? No. Am I sympathetic? Sure. But don't think that means I'm going to let you stir shit up just to save your job.

CHRIS. Honey, I don't need to stir shit up: we got a president throwing his feces at the wall.

JEAN. There isn't a story in Washington smutty enough to get you back in the game, Chris.

CHRIS. That a challenge?

JEAN. That's a warning.

CHRIS. First Lady still going to the gala tonight?

JEAN. Why wouldn't she?

CHRIS. Might be feeling a bit cunty.

JEAN. Don't use that language in my office, please

CHRIS. *Give it up, Jean*

JEAN. *Get off my dick, Chris.*

CHRIS. Is that your comment?

JEAN. Yes.

1.4

(**STEPHANIE** *vs.* **DUSTY.**)

(**STEPHANIE** *power-stances in the bathroom, earbuds in her ears, meekly singing along to an aggressive pop song from the BitchBeats playlist.* **DUSTY** *runs in and vomits in the trashcan. She clutches an oversized blue slushy.*)

STEPHANIE. Oh!

DUSTY. Frick. I'm so sorry.

STEPHANIE. Are you okay?

DUSTY. Frick, I got it on my sleeve.

STEPHANIE. Is that a normal color to be coming out of a person?

DUSTY. It was buy-one-get-one-half-off for blue raz slushies. There wasn't even a line!

STEPHANIE. Okay.

DUSTY. Slushies are the only thing I can eat right now. Everything else makes me totally sick. I was feeling great after the blushies – that's what I call blue raz slushies – and then I ate a baby carrot and it all went to frick.

STEPHANIE. Do you need a doctor?

DUSTY. Oh my gosh you're the cutest to worry, but I'm fine! It's for a beautiful reason! I'm pregnant!

---

*A license to produce *POTUS* does not include a performance license for any third-party or copyrighted music. Licensees should create an original composition or use music in the public domain. For further information, please see the Music and Third-Party Materials Use Note on page iii.

STEPHANIE. Wow. That is

>   (**DUSTY** *vomits blue.*)

beautiful.

DUSTY. Gross. Sorry. I didn't mean to interrupt your dance practice.

STEPHANIE. I / wasn't

DUSTY. Whatcha listening to? Oh my gosh – BitchBeats is my favorite playlist! You know they have a karaoke version?

>   (*She grabs one of* **STEPHANIE**'s *earbuds and starts loudly singing along.*)

STEPHANIE. Um, are you an intern?

DUSTY. (*Delighted.*) Oh my gosh do I look like an intern?

STEPHANIE. Not at all.

DUSTY. I'm just visiting.

STEPHANIE. Are you important or are you lost? Did you get separated from a tour? Sorry, it's just you're not allowed to be in this wing unless you have the proper clearance.

>   (**DUSTY** *holds up a pass.*)

DUSTY. I thought that's what this is for.

STEPHANIE. How did you get that? Who are you?

DUSTY. I'm Dusty.

>   ;

STEPHANIE. As in

DUSTY. Dusty.

STEPHANIE. Okay.

DUSTY. I'm here about the position.

> *(She winks.)*

STEPHANIE. What position?

DUSTY. The position.

> *(She winks again.)*

STEPHANIE. Why are you winking.

DUSTY. I was told to be *discreet.*

STEPHANIE. So why are you winking.

DUSTY. Do you mind just, like, pointing me towards the president?

STEPHANIE. *Point* you towards the *president*?

DUSTY. I feel dumb, this is all new to me. I'm supposed to tell the lady that I'm here about the position.

STEPHANIE. Which lady? What lady? The First Lady?

DUSTY. I can't remember her name, but she's, like, I don't know, she's like really intense?

STEPHANIE. *(Shrill.)* They're *all* intense here, *everyone's intense here*!

> **(CHRIS** *enters, on the phone, breastmilk leaking through her shirt.)*

CHRIS. Greg, I swear to god if you don't cancel your date and pick Kenny up from dance class tonight, I will feed our children nothing but prunes for the two days leading up to your weekend with them and they will blow ass on that new white leather couch you think makes your shitty studio look like a bachelor pad!

> *(Unable to mop up the stains, she shoves some paper towels into her bra and exits.)*

DUSTY. Not her, but *woah.*

STEPHANIE. Oh my god are you here for *my* position? Are they *firing* me?

DUSTY. No! I mean I don't know. I don't know who you / are

STEPHANIE. They're replacing ME with YOU? The girl who vomits BLUE?

DUSTY. Are you okay? You're rhyming.

STEPHANIE. How many languages do you speak?

DUSTY. I think just English.

> (**STEPHANIE** *frantically hits a power stance and attempts a breathing technique.* **DUSTY** *mirrors her.*)

If you arch your back more your boobs will look bigger. I was captain of my school's dance team.

> (*She demonstrates a brief but aggressive moment of choreo.*)

STEPHANIE. I'm gonna be sick.

DUSTY. (*Offering her drink.*) Blushie?

1.5

(**HARRIET** *on the phone, pacing.*)

HARRIET. Leslie, of course you still want the president's endorsement! You're running for governor! Just because a few FML guests

> (*From the TV:*)

> "...*have threatened to boycott tonight's White House dinner...*"

Okay, but no one's going to notice if

> (*From the TV:*)

> "...*the notoriously outspoken musician is now expressing hesitation to perform at the White House...*"

Look Jean's a pro, she's handling it, it's handled, they're already on to the next cycle

> (*Just as* **JEAN** *runs in, from the TV:*)

> "...*when approached for comment, an anonymous White House source responded, quote, 'Get off my dick.'*"

I have to go.

> (*She hangs up.*)

"GET OFF MY DICK"?

JEAN. I'm going to kill Chris

HARRIET. I'm going to kill YOU

JEAN. I was joking! She knew that! We have a rapport

HARRIET. I'm about to go into the non-proliferation meeting with forty world leaders, / I can't be dealing with this

JEAN. Just be aware that Bahrain is pissy.

HARRIET. What do you mean, Bahrain's pissy?

JEAN. About cunty! He's pissy about cunty!

HARRIET. So is everyone!

JEAN. He thought it was disrespectful.

HARRIET. *Oh did he?* Did he take a break from imprisoning journalists to issue that statement?

JEAN. I'm just saying POTUS has to be extra careful in there.

HARRIET. I don't have time for this! The whole point of these talks is reducing nuclear weapons among global powers – is Bahrain a global power?

JEAN. Depends on your definition of

HARRIET. No! The only reason Bahrain was even invited today was to look like we give a shit about tiny Arab countries

JEAN. *(Sarcastically.)* Nice, I love the smell of imperialism in the morning.

HARRIET. Oh shut up! Obviously we *personally* care that tiny Arab countries *exist*, we just don't *geopolitically* care if they're *pissy*

JEAN. *Other* countries might

HARRIET. Wow, Jean, I had no idea your BA in *marketing* made you such a fucking expert on international diplomacy!

JEAN. I'm talking about the optics, you shriveled twat! Turns out, nuclear war polls really badly with women. So if you want FML to actually land that voting block, POTUS has to *appear*, for *one day*, like a level-headed, peace-seeking

HARRIET. Okay well he will! He's great in these meetings. He thrives in these meetings. He's great in these meetings.

JEAN. You said great twice.

HARRIET. This is his wheelhouse. Room full of men, talking about weapons and war, not a woman in sight

JEAN. You'll be there.

HARRIET. Of course I'll be there.

JEAN. You're a woman.

HARRIET. I don't count.

JEAN. *(Kindly.)* Don't say that. I like your haircut. I don't think it's mannish at all.

HARRIET. What?

JEAN. Nothing.

HARRIET. Who said it was mannish?

JEAN. No one.

Nothing.

POTUS. But what does he know about

(**STEPHANIE** *careens into the room.*)

STEPHANIE. Dusty girl there's a Dusty girl Dusty in the bathroom

JEAN. Just rinse her off.

STEPHANIE. No it's her name her name's Dusty and she's throwing up but says she's here about the position?

HARRIET. Oh my god. She's not supposed to be here until 3:30!

STEPHANIE. *(Edge of tears.)* So you *do* have a meeting with her? You *are* considering her?

HARRIET. Bring the girl to my office. Don't let anyone talk to her.

JEAN. Who is she?

HARRIET. No one.

Nothing.

Don't you have a situation to be containing right now?

JEAN. If there's something you need to tell me

HARRIET. How about *"Get off my dick!"*

JEAN. Okay I'm going!

    (She exits.)

HARRIET. FUCK SHIT BALLS Don't panic.

    (To **STEPHANIE.***)* Find something for the president to sit on. At dinner. Something that allows him to / sit

STEPHANIE. Like a chair?

HARRIET. No, *not* like a chair

STEPHANIE. But maybe a chair with, like, a hole in it or, like, maybe an inner tube! You know, one of those floaty

HARRIET. I know what an inner tube is

STEPHANIE. If we covered it with fabric

HARRIET. Do I look like a sounding board to you, Stephanie?

STEPHANIE. No, Ma'am

HARRIET. Find the First Lady and tell her I need her smiling next to POTUS at the Leslie Hopper endorsement. I don't care what you do to get her there, just get her there

STEPHANIE. Oh god

HARRIET. But bring the girl to my office

STEPHANIE. What do I do first

HARRIET. *All of them Stephanie I need all of them first!* Look at me. Look at me. Look at me: if there was ever a time to prove your worth It. Is. Now. Do you understand?

> *(Flinging herself into a power stance, about to weep:)*

STEPHANIE. Yes, Ma'am!

HARRIET. This is your job. Are you good at your job?

STEPHANIE. I am good at my / job!

HARRIET. You are woman! Hear you roar!

> *(Terrified and deeply inspired,* **STEPHANIE** *releases something half-roar, half-wail:)*

STEPHANIE. AAAAAAAAAH

HARRIET. Don't actually yell, Stephanie, there / are meetings

STEPHANIE. I'm so sorry

HARRIET. *Why are you still standing there?*

STEPHANIE. I just wanted to say how much I've loved working here and how much I appreciate all of your mentorship

HARRIET. GO.

> *(**STEPHANIE** flees.)*

1.6

(A room with two doors on opposite sides. The stage-right door leads to a hallway, the stage-left door leads to an adjoining office. A closet up-center. A few valuable and unnecessary objects displayed around, including a delicate vase, an antique musket, and a heavy bust.)

(**CHRIS** *vs.* **MARGARET.**)

MARGARET. Well there is no typical, Chris. My daily work is determined by the ever-shifting needs of my five non-profits, two children, and of course, one and only president.

> (**CHRIS** *is holding the recording device out with one hand while holding her jacket closed over breastmilk stains with the other. Her phone buzzes.)*

CHRIS. Sorry, my babysitter's

MARGARET. If you need to take that

CHRIS. No, no. Please continue.

MARGARET. The truth is, even before I was First Lady I always wore multiple hats. Granted, I only had three non-profits back then, but after graduating from Stanford and then Harvard, I managed to keep busy enough with my law firm, my husband's campaigns, my campaigns, my talk show, my book, my other book, my cookbook, my gallery and Taekwondo.

> (**CHRIS**'*phone buzzes. She twitches but doesn't look at it.)*

If you want to

CHRIS. Nope. All the women we are interviewing for this series excel in their respective fields, but you have broken glass ceilings in so many different areas.

MARGARET. You're too kind

CHRIS. Politically, culturally, philanthropically

MARGARET. Joyful work

CHRIS. *(Joking.)* Why aren't *you* president?

MARGARET. *(Joking.)* That's the eternal question, isn't it?

(They laugh gaily for a moment, then fall into dismal silence.)

CHRIS. / Anyway

MARGARET. Anyway

CHRIS. How do you decompress after a long day?

MARGARET. You're a mother, Chris, so you know there is nothing more relaxing than spending time with your family

(As her phone buzzes:)

CHRIS. So relaxing.

MARGARET. But also, I hunt!

CHRIS. Hunt. As in

MARGARET. My Ladies Big Game Hunting Club! For ladies who love to hunt! You should join! Nothing helps you cast off a hard day like stalking your prey, listening for the slightest crack, sniffing for that faintest whiff of musky, gamey smell – and then once you have the beast in your crosshairs, feeling the force of the gun as you pull the trigger, and squinting in the hopes of seeing that splash of blood, that moment of animal shock, as the bullet enters the creature, penetrates the flesh, snuffing out his small, mediocre life once and for all.

;

CHRIS. That is, um, really

MARGARET. Earthy.

CHRIS. Right. You've spent your three years in the White House focusing your energy on child hunger

MARGARET. *(Revving up for her grand speech.)* Yes, and when I think of the ten million children living in poverty

CHRIS. Totally. And since seventy-one percent of those kids are children of color, I was wondering if you had any plans to spend your last year in office

MARGARET. Before reelection

CHRIS. *(Over her.)* Using your position as a Black First Lady to push our president towards addressing systemic issues impacting the Black community and marginalized groups in general?

MARGARET. *(Through a tense smile.)* Well, Chris, perhaps *you* consider your Black readers a monolith

CHRIS. *(Through a tense smile.)* That's not what I

MARGARET. *(Over her.)* But I have spent a lifetime fighting that kind of generalization by subverting stereotypes, rejecting identity politics, and being, across the board, un-fucking-paralleled.

CHRIS. *(Briskly.)* Right, so was that a "no" on, say, Black maternal health, voting rights, abolition, reparations

MARGARET. Sounds like you got your stump speech! Maybe *you* should run for president.

CHRIS. Ha! – I would if I wasn't still paying off the hospital bills for my C-section. Speaking of cunty

> **(STEPHANIE** *careens into the room, carrying a large inner tube.)*

STEPHANIE. CHRIST Chris hi Chris, good to see you, sorry to interrupt, I was just

(Remembering the inner tube.) Oh, this?

MARGARET. Stephanie

STEPHANIE. This is a, um, gift for the First Lady. From the staff

MARGARET. Stephanie

STEPHANIE. Because um, everyone knows she loves inner tubing. Because of how. Earthy. She is.

MARGARET. *Stephanie. A word.*

> *(She drags* **STEPHANIE** *into the next room.)*
>
> *(Meanwhile, in the hallway, as* **JEAN** *rushes past...)*

DUSTY. Wait, hi, hi, I know you, you're on TV!

JEAN. Okay.

DUSTY. I'm a little confused.

JEAN. Ask one of the other interns, / I can't

DUSTY. Could you just point me towards the president?

JEAN. What?

DUSTY. I'm Dusty.

JEAN. I can't help you with that.

DUSTY. No, I'm Dusty.

JEAN. *(Realizing.)* That's your name.

DUSTY. Yes.

JEAN. Why is your mouth blue?

DUSTY. Blushies. I'm pregnant.

JEAN. Who are you?

DUSTY. I'm Dusty.

JEAN. You're meeting with Harriet?

DUSTY. Is she the intense one?

JEAN. She's a walking Kegel.

DUSTY. Do you know when the president will be ready to see me? I know he has a lot going on, but I'm only here until tomorrow night and then I'm flying back to the farm.

JEAN. The farm.

DUSTY. In Iowa.

JEAN. You're a farmer from Iowa.

DUSTY. Well my dad's the real farmer, but I can handle a hoe. The dream is to start my own regenerative ranch

JEAN. *(Struggling to comprehend.)* Hang on

DUSTY. Can I show you the vision board?

JEAN. You're the daughter of a farmer and you're meeting with Harriet but you're here to see the president.

DUSTY. He sent a private jet!

JEAN. And you're pregnant.

DUSTY. Eighteen weeks! Big as a bell pepper.

          ;

JEAN. *(With dawning horror.)* Are you by any chance into rough ass play?

DUSTY. *(Thoughtfully.)* I guess I am sometimes.

JEAN. *(Spiraling out.)* Holy fucking balls shit ass bucket / pissing dick

DUSTY. Actually I'm trying not to expose the baby to unkind sounds, / so if you could

JEAN. Cock-sucking fuck me with a flaming screwdriver

BERNADETTE. Now that takes me back.

> (**JEAN** *whirls around.* **BERNADETTE***'s standing there in cargo shorts and a trench coat, an overstuffed duffel slung over one shoulder, an ankle monitor on her leg, and a lit cigarette in her hand.*)

JEAN. *Bernadette*

BERNADETTE. SURPRISE! Jeanie, baby, how are you! What's *happening*? Fuck, what a dump. You gotta start hiring hotter interns – all your staff look like sweaty Beanie Babies. *(Aggressively to a passing intern.)* YOU: coffee. Seven sugars, dash of triple sec.

DUSTY. Sorry, but would you mind putting out your cigarette? I'm pregnant.

BERNADETTE. And I'm constipated. We all have our trials.

> *(To* **JEAN**.*)* Who's the Prosti-Tot?

DUSTY. I'm Dusty.

BERNADETTE. What'd you do – blow a Smurf?

JEAN. What's happening how is this happening

BERNADETTE. I banged one of those Blue Man guys once – you know, in my experimental phase: stamina like a bull but I was queefing cobalt for days.

JEAN. You're in PRISON!

BERNADETTE. *Was* in prison.

DUSTY. Has anyone ever told you you look so much like the president? Like, you could be his sister.

BERNADETTE. Holy tits, he's screwing her, isn't he?

DUSTY. / Actually the president and I are in love, so it's a lot more than just

JEAN. LOWER your voice, oh my god keep it down SHUT UP.

(*To* **BERNADETTE.**) How are you here?

BERNADETTE. My presidential pardon, baby!

JEAN. For the last time, he's not going to pardon you!

BERNADETTE. Babe, he basically already has. Pulled some strings with the warden and judge so I could get out today, and so long as he makes it official in the next twenty-four hours, they cut this ankle shit off and then it's free Bernie howling at the moon all night every night Ow OWWWWW – give me a howl Prosti-Tot!

DUSTY. Ow / OWWWWWWW

BERNADETTE. Ow / OWWWWWWWW

JEAN. Stop it STOP howling NO HOWLING in the White House!

DUSTY. She's so FUN!

BERNADETTE. (*Viciously, to a passerby.*) Yo, what you looking at? Did I say you could film me, bitch? / I will cut that phone out of your hand

JEAN. They're *fifth-graders* – they're on a *field trip*!

Listen to me: I don't know what "sibling bond" bullshit you fed POTUS to guilt him into this one but there is no way anyone here is letting him pardon an international drug mule

BERNADETTE. (*Winking at* **DUSTY.**) I prefer "drug *stallion*."

JEAN. You're not seeing him.

BERNADETTE. That's not up to you.

JEAN. It's up to Harriet, which is why I know you're not seeing him.

BERNADETTE. Harriet works for my brother.

JEAN. Harriet *works* your brother. Harriet's the number one reason this country continues to function.

BERNADETTE. So why isn't she president?

JEAN. That's the eternal question, isn't it?

DUSTY. Is she the one with the man's haircut?

JEAN. *(At* **DUSTY.***)* Don't

BERNADETTE. This is a bitter fucking welcome, you know that? You know how many favors I had to call in just so I could see you today on our anniversary?

DUSTY. Awwww

JEAN. Ex-anniversary! And the only reason you ever do *anything* is for you and if you think I'm going to fall for your star-crossed lovers, Bonnie and Clyde bullshit

(**BERNADETTE** *slowly backs* **JEAN** *up.)*

BERNADETTE. Come on, Jeanie. Those were some long, wet nights on the campaign trail. Don't tell me you've forgotten

JEAN. *(Struggling to stay strong.)* I-I-I'm not saying I've forgotten, / I just

BERNADETTE. Prison changed me. I'm looking for commitment and intimacy, a second chance at life and love. I mean, think of what this pardon could mean for *us.*

JEAN. *(Melting.)* Us?

BERNADETTE. I missed you.

JEAN. Did you?

BERNADETTE. You look great.

JEAN. Do I?

BERNADETTE. Love the suit.

JEAN. Do you?

BERNADETTE. Very Jackie O meets Carl Sagan.

JEAN. *(Humbly.)* Turtlenecks are universally flattering.

BERNADETTE. Let's get out of here

DUSTY. *(Thrilled for them.)* Do it.

JEAN. Okay yes I mean yes I mean yes – NO! That's it. Bernie, go to my office – Wait. No. Dusty, *you* go to my – No. Bad. / Okay okay

BERNADETTE. You seem stressed.

DUSTY. I think you're the intense one.

JEAN. Give me your / bag, give me your

BERNADETTE. Watch it – I got breakables in there

JEAN. What are these?

BERNADETTE. What do they look like? Tums.

> *(Handing the container of "Tums" to* **DUSTY***:)*

JEAN. Hold this

DUSTY. Can I have one?

JEAN. / No.

BERNADETTE. No.

> *(***JEAN*** pins* **BERNADETTE** *hard against the wall and starts roughly patting her down.)*

For / fuck's sake

JEAN. You're not going anywhere until I know you're clean.

> *(***BERNADETTE*** turns, flipping them once again and bracing a leg against the wall so that* **JEAN** *is now pinned.)*

BERNADETTE. I'm a new woman, Jean: clean as a whistle, straight as an edge. So you can strip me down and turn me inside out, but all you're gonna find is pure, fine, fresh Bernie.

> (**JEAN** *reaches up* **BERNADETTE***'s shorts and pulls out a Ziploc bag of cash.*)

DUSTY. *(Thrilled.)* Where was that? I have so many questions!

BERNADETTE. Okay, so here's the thing...

> (*Meanwhile:* **MARGARET** *vs.* **STEPHANIE.** **STEPHANIE** *clutches the inner tube.*)

STEPHANIE.	MARGARET.
I understand you are upset, Ma'am, Margaret, Margie, but this is not coming from me, it's coming from POTUS, or, or rather, Harriet, and I'm afraid it is non-negotiable – I hear you, but you are expected to accompany POTUS to the	This interview is about ME! Not my husband, not the presidency – ME, and Harriet can gnash her teeth about my popularity all she wants but I will not allow her to ruin this by sending some spineless, sweaty, saltine of a human to

> (**STEPHANIE** *finally snaps. In power stance:*)

STEPHANIE. AAAAAAAAAAAAH you will accompany POTUS to the front lawn. You will stand next to him and you will smile DON'T TEST ME I AM GOOD AT MY JOB

> (**HARRIET** *enters.*)

HARRIET. What the hell is going on here?

> (*Crumpling to the ground:*)

STEPHANIE. Oh thank god

MARGARET. *(To* **HARRIET.***)* If you have things to say to me, Harry, you tell me directly, don't send your Pomeranian to piddle on my shoe.

HARRIET. Don't worry, Marge, throw those shoes in the dishwasher and they'll be good as new.

MARGARET. Contain your minion!

HARRIET. What'd you do to her?

MARGARET. Nothing!

HARRIET. Stand up, Stephanie.

STEPHANIE. I can't.

HARRIET. Get up, Stephanie.

STEPHANIE. Not yet.

HARRIET. Now, Stephanie!

STEPHANIE. It's better down here.

> *(Back in the interview room:* **CHRIS***, alone, is trying to mop up breastmilk stains while talking in hushed tones on the phone.)*

CHRIS. No, she just stepped out for a second, but I'm telling you

> *(The sound of* **STEPHANIE** *breaking down, offstage.)*

there is some crazy shit going down here – No! Don't send Nate! I'm saying I got this – hang on, that's my babysitter – don't send Nate!

> *(She switches calls.)*

Hi, Lucy, if you go into the garage there should be extra wipes in a box labeled "Emergency Baby."

> *(***HARRIET** *opens the door and pokes her head in.* **STEPHANIE** *is momentarily visible*

in the doorway behind her, curled in the fetal position on the floor, whimpering, as **MARGARET** *stands over her, berating the girl.)*

HARRIET. Chris, hi, we'll just be another five.

*(She slams the door in **CHRIS**'s face.)*

CHRIS. *(To her babysitter.)* I have to go. Figure it out!

*(**CHRIS** checks her watch, rips off her jacket, snatches up the breast pump, and scrambles to put it on. She manages to get her shirt off and the pump partially on when **JEAN**'s voice becomes audible in the hallway. **CHRIS** frantically ducks into the closet with only her phone and breast pump – closing the door just as **JEAN** enters, dragging **BERNADETTE** and **DUSTY**.)*

JEAN. Are you kidding? This is unbelievable. You get out of prison this MORNING and you are already selling drugs in my White House?

BERNADETTE. It's temporary! Just a little fast cash while I'm getting back on my feet.

DUSTY. *(Nodding somberly.)* We really need to put more resources into rehabilitation if we're ever going to tackle recidivism.

JEAN. *(Aggressively, at **DUSTY**.)* Don't you have a prostate to stimulate?

DUSTY. Well if you could point me towards the president

JEAN. No!

BERNADETTE. Look I wasn't even selling today, just collecting on some deals while I was in town

JEAN. "SOME DEALS"

BERNADETTE. No drugs exchanged hands on these grounds. We have a system where I

JEAN. A "SYSTEM"? Who the fuck is "WE"?

BERNADETTE. You know I can't breach the confidentiality of my clients

JEAN. If you don't tell me right now I'm going to shove / this bag so far up your uterus

DUSTY. Violent violent this feels violent

BERNADETTE. It's not even bad stuff, mostly pharmaceuticals that are already legal in some countries

JEAN. I want names

BERNADETTE. Russia, parts of India

JEAN. *Names of the people you sell to*

BERNADETTE. I don't know – Marcus, Lance, Jack, / Jake, Sheldon, Kyle

JEAN. That's half the Cabinet! I'm gonna kill 'em I'm gonna stab 'em in the taint

DUSTY. Ma'am, I'm going to need you to take a deep breath

JEAN. YOUR NAME IS AN ADJECTIVE: DON'T TELL ME WHAT TO DO.

> *(The office door opens.* **HARRIET, MARGARET,** *and* **STEPHANIE** *stare at them from the doorway.)*

HARRIET. Jean?

JEAN. Harry

MARGARET. Bernie

BERNADETTE. Marge

STEPHANIE. *(A wail of despair, at* **DUSTY.**) YOU?

DUSTY. *(Helpfully, pointing at her chest and enunciating slowly.)* Dusty.

MARGARET. Oh my god she broke out of prison to kill us all!

BERNADETTE. Like I'd waste a manicure snapping your leathery neck. I got a guy for that.

MARGARET. I should have known you were here by the smell of lies and yeast infection.

> *(Yanking a large, silver candlestick holder out of her duffel and advancing on* **MARGARET**:*)*

BERNADETTE. Hey, I paid extra for non-chip nails so let's go

MARGARET. That's *my* candlestick holder!

BERNADETTE. Then you shouldn't have left it out on the table for anyone to take!

HARRIET. *(To* **JEAN**.*)* This is you containing the situation?

JEAN. *(To* **HARRIET**.*)* Do NOT lecture me

MARGARET. *(To* **BERNADETTE**.*)* Get out of my White House, or I will tell your mother you're here

BERNADETTE. You wouldn't voluntarily call that hag for anything. The only one she hates more than me, is you.

JEAN. YOU are Chief of Staff: YOUR job is to contain situations. I'M the PRESS SECRETARY

MARGARET. If you've stolen so much as a fork from the White House – Stephanie, check her bag.

STEPHANIE. Yes, / Ma'am

BERNADETTE. *(To* **STEPHANIE**.*)* Put a hand on me, kid, I bite it off.

STEPHANIE. Yes, / Ma'am

JEAN. MY job is to contain STORIES and I can't contain stories if I don't KNOW the SITUATION, so perhaps you'd like to explain THIS SITUATION

> *(She waves* DUSTY's *arm in the air – the one still holding the bottle of "Tums."* BERNADETTE *reaches for the container, but* JEAN *intercepts and shoves the bottle into* STEPHANIE's *hands.)*

HARRIET. Put Dusty in my office, Stephanie

STEPHANIE. Yes, / Ma'am

JEAN. Stay where you are, Stephanie

STEPHANIE. Yes, Ma'am

BERNADETTE. *(To* MARGARET.*)* You got some nerve greeting me like this. You know, I spent an hour on the phone with your son yesterday explaining why it's bad to use tanning lotion as lube.

HARRIET. *(Staring* JEAN *down.)* Now, Stephanie

STEPHANIE. / Yes Ma'am

JEAN. *(Staring* HARRIET *down.)* Don't move, Stephanie

STEPHANIE. *(Hyperventilating.)* Oh my god

> *(*STEPHANIE *frantically pops a couple "Tums" into her mouth.)*

MARGARET. Marley would never be so crude

BERNADETTE. Why, 'cause he comes from such classy parentage? Sorry to hear about your morning, Marge, I'm afraid I'm all out of cunty pills

> *(*DUSTY *takes control of the situation: A rap. With sexy choreography.)*

DUSTY.

> HEY THERE, FRIEND, WHAT'D YOU SAY?
> YOU SAY YOU'RE HAVING A REAL BAD DAY?
> LET'S SIT DOWN AND CHAT AWHILE
> WE'LL FIND A WAY TO MAKE YOU SMILE
> 'CAUSE CONFLICT CAN BE HEALTHY
> CONFLICT CAN BE TRUE
> CONFLICT CAN BRING ME CLOSER TO YOU
> SO LET'S COGITATE AND ARTICULATE
> DON'T MONOLOGUE, LET'S DIALOGUE
> BUT IN ORDER TO GROW, FIRST WE MUST LISTEN
> AND IN ORDER TO LISTEN
> FIRST WE MUST HUSH
> FIRST WE MUST HUSH
> FIRST WE MUST HUSHHH

> *(Silence. They stare at her.* **DUSTY** *nods encouragingly.)*

That's great, guys, really good stuff.

BERNADETTE. I've dropped acid on Air Force One on three separate occasions but that was by far the most out-of-body experience I've ever had.

STEPHANIE. *(At* **HARRIET.**) HER? SERIOUSLY?

MARGARET. *(Re:* **DUSTY.**) What is this?

DUSTY. It seems like there are a lot of strong feelings in the room right now, but the good news is I am a certified conflict resolution mediator and I'm happy to provide my services.

STEPHANIE. *(Desperately.)* I could be a mediator! I'll get certified! I'll do whatever you want!

> *(Everyone is now looking at* **STEPHANIE,** *except for* **MARGARET,** *who continues to stare at* **DUSTY.**)*

HARRIET. What are you / talking about?

STEPHANIE. You don't have to fire me I'll take up space I'll mediate while taking up space

HARRIET. Stephanie, what the fuck is / going on with you –

> *(Eyes fixed on* **DUSTY**, *with the cold, calm dawning of understanding:)*

MARGARET. Oh my god you're the one into ass play, aren't you?

> ;

DUSTY. Why do people keep asking me that? Is it my highlights?

BERNADETTE. She's into more than that: you don't get pregnant off ass play.

MARGARET. / *Pregnant?*

HARRIET. Bernadette, / for the love of

STEPHANIE. *(Crying.)* I could be into ass play! If that's what you want, I could, I could

> *(She frantically chews a few more "Tums.")*

JEAN. / Wait, no

BERNADETTE. Oh, shit

> *(***BERNADETTE*** snatches the "Tums" from* **STEPHANIE.***)*

JEAN. How many of those have you had?

STEPHANIE. Six?

BERNADETTE. *Oh shit*

JEAN. Don't say oh shit they're Tums Bernie tell me they're Tums

MARGARET. *(Advancing on* **DUSTY**.*)* Listen to me, you little slut

HARRIET. No / no no no

BERNADETTE. Look, everyone responds differently, she might not even feel them

STEPHANIE. Feel what?

MARGARET. If you think you can show up here, unannounced, / and blackmail the president

STEPHANIE. Feel what?

DUSTY. What? No, POTUS *invited* me, I'm here to celebrate our little president-to-be.

MARGARET. NOPE, that's it, I'm out – BERNIE.

> (**BERNADETTE** *tosses her the "Tums."* **MARGARET** *dry-swallows two and lies down on the floor.*)

JEAN. *Are you kidding me?*

BERNADETTE. Relax, those things are like vitamins to her by now.

STEPHANIE. *(Hazily.)* Are my feet on the ground?

BERNADETTE. / Oh shit.

JEAN. Oh shit.

DUSTY. When I sent him a pic of the ultrasound he texted me that I should come in to celebrate.

HARRIET. Nope, that was me.

DUSTY. What? No, 'cause then I also sent him my favorite Rilke poem and a picture of my nipples.

HARRIET. And they were great. The thing is, POTUS is really busy. He's actually going into a meeting about *bombs* in

> (*She checks her watch.*)

seven minutes ago, fuck me – so he's talking to world leaders about bombs, *right now*, sweetie, and I'm actually supposed to be in there with him, so you and I are just gonna have a quick little chat / and

JEAN. Here? You're doing this IN the White House?

HARRIET. Where else am I gonna do it? A back alley? You don't think that'd make her a bit suspicious?

JEAN. Have you TALKED to the girl? You could tell her to meet you at the ABORTION CLINIC and she wouldn't be suspicious!

DUSTY. *(Cheerfully.)* I volunteer at a clinic back in Iowa. Affordable, safe reproductive health care is a basic human right.

STEPHANIE. *(Anxious.) Where is the ground?*

HARRIET. Okay, honey? Honey, here's the thing: as much fun as I'm sure you and the president had together

DUSTY. We're in love.

> (**MARGARET** *cackles bitterly from the floor.*)

HARRIET. The thing is this pregnancy is not, um. Happening.

DUSTY. It is, I have a copy of the ultrasound right here.

HARRIET. Ooh I'll take that.

> *(She passes the picture to* **JEAN,** *who immediately rips it up.)*

So, um, there are a few options, or, really just two options. There's adoption. Which is great. Jean's kid is adopted

JEAN. *(To* **HARRIET.***)* Please don't / bring me in

HARRIET. See? Your baby could have a mom like Jean! Isn't Jean great?

DUSTY. The violent one with no neck?

JEAN. Turtlenecks are universally

HARRIET. *(To* **JEAN.**) Shut the fuck up. *(Back to* **DUSTY,** *sugary sweet.)* So adoption's one option and obviously we would handle all the logistics there. Um and the other option is, ummmm, not doing it at all.

DUSTY. And the other option is having it.

HARRIET. I feel like we're not quite understanding each other.

BERNADETTE. She means snip, snip, flush

HARRIET. *Jesus / Christ*

BERNADETTE. I'm on a clock here, I got a pardon to get!

HARRIET. *(Back to* **DUSTY.**) See, the way it works is we give you money and, in exchange, the pregnancy isn't – it doesn't – it it it goes away.

DUSTY. Thank you, but I don't need money. Our farm's the number-one flax farm in Iowa.

STEPHANIE. *There is no ground! Why is there no ground?*

HARRIET. *(To* **DUSTY.**) Okay honey, honey, we're talking about the President of the United States, right? The *married* president

    (**MARGARET** *cackles bitterly.*)

Do you see the problem? Do you see how that could make for some icky headlines?

DUSTY. I guess I do see why a few people might be mad about the president having a baby with someone other than his wife

HARRIET. Good, good, I'm glad you see / that.

DUSTY. *(Thoughtful.)* But I kinda think *more* people would be even *madder* if they found out you tried to bribe the president's girlfriend into having an abortion against her will. Don't you think?

(From the closet, the loud, rhythmic hum of a breast pump. A confused moment where they all try to locate the source.)

STEPHANIE. *(Terrified.)* The walls are BREATHING!

(HARRIET crosses to the door and yanks it open: CHRIS, huddled in the closet, topless but for the breast pump, holding her phone up to record everything. A moment of frozen shock. As the "Tums" hit STEPHANIE with full force:)

(Pointing in horror at CHRIS's breast pump.) DEVIL BOOBS!

(And she drops to the floor. CHRIS seizes the opportunity to make a run for it.)

MARGARET. GET HER

(Pandemonium ensues. It's a wild and epic chase, with much leaping and tackling and tripping over STEPHANIE's limp body.)

JEAN. I GOT HER PHONE

HARRIET. DON'T LET HER LEAVE

(BERNADETTE dives in front of the door to the hallway. MARGARET runs at CHRIS, screaming, a chair held aloft. CHRIS grabs the vase and throws it at MARGARET. DUSTY snatches it out of the air just in time.)

MARGARET. That is twelfth-century Japan you uncultured cow!

(CHRIS seizes the bust and, with great effort, raises it over her head.)

NO NO NO

CHRIS. Give me my phone and get out of my way or I will break this head into a million pieces

MARGARET. That is notable suffragist Alice Paul!

CHRIS. I will break her ugly face!

JEAN. Break whatever you want you're not getting your phone!

(From the floor, **STEPHANIE** *rouses slightly:)*

STEPHANIE. "...Took my pride away-eeay-eeay-eeayyyy"

CHRIS. One

MARGARET. NO

CHRIS. Two

HARRIET. Wait

CHRIS. THREE

*(***JEAN*** throws* **CHRIS***'s phone to the floor, smashing it.* **CHRIS** *hurls the bust across the room just as the office door opens.* **MARGARET** *and* **HARRIET** *duck.* **BERNADETTE** *pulls* **JEAN** *down.* **DUSTY** *covers* **STEPHANIE***. The bust sails through the doorway.)*

(Offstage, there is the thunk of the bust colliding with an unseen person's head – then the thud of a body hitting the floor. Silence.)

HARRIET. ...Mr. President?

(Blackout. Intermission.)

ACT II

2.1

*(Thirty seconds later. Each **WOMAN** exactly where she was, frozen in shock, staring through the open door into the office at the body on the ground. The office, and the body within it, are never visible, but anyone who passes through that door turns sideways so as not to step on the body. A moment, then:)*

DUSTY. NOOOOOOOOOOOOOOOO

(She runs toward the body. **HARRIET** *tackles her, pinning her to the ground, trying to smother her wailing.)*

BERNADETTE. Oh HELL no

CHRIS. Oh my god / oh my god oh my god oh my god oh my god

DUSTY. *(Sobbing.)* MY LOVVVVVVVE HE'S DEEAAAAAAAD

HARRIET. Shut up shut up shut up

*(**BERNADETTE** has pulled rubber gloves and maxi pads out of her bag.)*

JEAN. What are you doing?

BERNADETTE. I'm wiping down fingerprints, and then you and me, we're skipping town, we're going to Mongolia

JEAN. *Mongolia?*

BERNADETTE. I got a guy!

DUSTY. YOU KILLED HIM

HARRIET. BE QUIET

>   *(**HARRIET** slaps **DUSTY**.)*

JEAN. Harriet!

>   *(**DUSTY** decks **HARRIET**.)*

/ Oh my god!

BERNADETTE. *Damn* she's got an arm

CHRIS. I'm going to go away for life they're going to send me to Guantanamo

DUSTY. YOU AND YOUR MEAN FRIENDS KILLED MY MY MY LOOOOOVE

>   *(Aggressively wrestling **DUSTY**:)*

HARRIET. Help me someone fucking help me

JEAN. *(To **HARRIET**.)* Don't hurt her! We can't kill another

CHRIS. They'll give the kids to Greg and then one of his girlfriends will put them up for adoption

DUSTY.   WE WERE GOING TO GROW FLAX TOGETHERRRRRR

>   *(**BERNADETTE** snatches the cardigan off **STEPHANIE**'s limp body; **STEPHANIE** stirs and starts sleepily pulling off her shirt as well. **BERNADETTE** shoves the cardigan into **DUSTY**'s mouth, tying it around her head, silencing her. **DUSTY** continues struggling toward the body, dragging **HARRIET** along.)*

CHRIS. They'll end up with those foster parents you read about, the ones who lock kids up in basements and make them into slaves

HARRIET. Stop – OW – *does it look like we have this under control, Jean?*

(**JEAN** *seizes* **STEPHANIE** *and pulls off her pants;* **STEPHANIE** *finds this delightful.*)

STEPHANIE. *(Sing-song.)*
NAKED TIIIMMME NAKED TIIIMMMME

(**JEAN** *uses* **STEPHANIE***'s pants to tie* **DUSTY***'s legs together.*)

CHRIS. They'll grow up to be psychopaths and I'll read about the kids *they* murder! / I'll read about their murders from my cell

JEAN. *(To* **DUSTY.***)* I'm / sorry but we can't let you go until you stop shouting

HARRIET. *(To* **DUSTY.***)* You have to shut up or we're all finished, do you understand me

(*Throughout this whole thing,* **MARGARET** *has not moved, except perhaps to shift her gaze from the body in the office to the chaos around her. Now, she crosses to* **DUSTY** *and grabs the girl by the shoulders, bringing them nose to nose.*)

MARGARET. *ENOUGH!* You say you loved him, yes? And he loved you? WHEN did he love you? When you were weak and weepy, on your back, girly and soft? NO! He loved you when you were an AMAZON, a BEAST, an EVIL STEPMOTHER shoving a TENNIS RACKET UP HIS ASS! So for the man you loved, the country he led, and the child he gave you, PULL YOURSELF TOGETHER.

(**DUSTY** *is silent and still.* **MARGARET** *releases her.*)

MARGARET. Bernie, untie her. Chris, stand up. Jean, go out the office door, tell the secret service that the president is going to be a bit.

CHRIS. A *bit*? He's going to be more than *a bit*

MARGARET. Oh I'm sorry, do you have a better idea? Is this all part of some master plan? Because here I thought your contribution ended at DEATH by DISCUS!

>   (**STEPHANIE** *puts the inner tube on like a tutu and becomes a ballerina.*)

BERNADETTE. She's right. Jean: go.

JEAN. Why me?

BERNADETTE. Because you lie for a living!

JEAN. I look at the bright side for a living!

HARRIET. Well right now you're going to go LIE!

CHRIS. This isn't going to work.

MARGARET. *(On the phone.)* Leslie, hi, in light of the concerns you expressed this morning, we've decided that the optics will be better if I do your endorsement and we push it back an hour.

HARRIET. *Now, Jean,* before we go down in history next to Booth and Oswald!

MARGARET. Wonderful, Leslie, we'll be in touch.

JEAN. What do I tell them?

HARRIET. Just buy us some time! Say anything! Say Margaret's giving him a blowjob

MARGARET. They'll never believe that.

BERNADETTE. Who's out there?

HARRIET. Two secret service agents: Kevin and

BERNADETTE. Kevin's a client.

HARRIET. Good, you go. Tell him FLOTUS and POTUS are doing something weird, say it's nasty, say he doesn't want to go in there.

MARGARET. Tell him it's the mango thing. Kevin's walked in on that one before.

DUSTY. *(Mournfully.)* He loved the mango thing.

HARRIET. If it doesn't work, give the guy drugs, give him money, give *him* a blowjob

CHRIS. *This is insane.*

BERNADETTE. Wait, who's the other one – is it Danny?

JEAN. Who cares?

BERNADETTE. We got bad blood.

JEAN. *Bad blood?*

BERNADETTE. He thinks I sold him some bad stuff and overcharged him for it.

JEAN. *Did you?*

BERNADETTE. The lines are blurry!

JEAN. You can't even *deal* drugs honestly? See, this is why you and I will never work

BERNADETTE. Hey, I'm *trying* to go legit and save up for my tattoo parlor but it's a tough economy right now because SOMEONE keeps NOT DELIVERING on his TAX PLAN!

HARRIET. That is CONGRESS! That is NOT our fault!

DUSTY. *(Nobly.)* I'll do it. I'll blow Kevin and Danny. For POTUS, I'll blow them both.

MARGARET. Atta girl.

(They high-five, grim.)

CHRIS. We are talking about the secret service here! They're not going to be sucked in by some kid trying to suck 'em off

BERNADETTE. Is she like the last idealistic journalist in Washington?

CHRIS. This is a matter of national security! We need to notify the vice president right now.

JEAN. Are you out of your / mind?

HARRIET. You've got to be / joking.

MARGARET. That man is as useful in a crisis as a turnip.

CHRIS. Someone ELSE, then. We need a PLAN. Dusty can deep throat her way through the White House, but that won't change the fact that we MURDERED the PRESIDENT

JEAN. You mean YOU murdered the president

> **(CHRIS** *snaps. With the rousing fury of a mother unleashed:)*

CHRIS. DON'T. YOU. DARE. If he was doing his job he would be across the White House right now making peace treaties! Why was he even here? He should not have walked in this room, he should not be living in this house, he should not be running this nation, and YOU KNOW IT! He's the pyromaniac, but *you* gave him kindling, you gave him matches, you figured he'd burn his fingers and learn his lesson – Well he DIDN'T, and now the WHOLE FUCKING WORLD IS ON FIRE! So we will douse those flames, or we will burn in them together, but don't think for one second I am marching to that stake by myself!

DUSTY. *(Deeply inspired.)* Holy frick, why isn't SHE president?

CHRIS. *(To* **DUSTY.***)* Go blow the secret service, kid!

DUSTY. How long do you need?

CHRIS. How long can you buy us?

DUSTY. *(Calculating.)* Fifteen minutes each, plus flirting and soothing – I'd say forty minutes total?

CHRIS. Make it forty-five.

DUSTY. I'll ask them about their favorite video games.

> (**DUSTY** *does a military salute and exits, head high, doing some vocal warm-ups.*)

CHRIS. *What. Is. Our. Plan.*

BERNADETTE. I have my plan, I'm getting out – Jeanie, let's go

JEAN. I have a kid!

BERNADETTE. We can ship him later!

JEAN. Ship him *how*?

BERNADETTE. I got a guy!

MARGARET. You are not going anywhere.

BERNADETTE. You gonna stop me, Marge?

> (**MARGARET** *pulls the musket off the wall and aims it at* **BERNADETTE.***)*

MARGARET. Yes.

BERNADETTE. That thing's not loaded.

MARGARET. Yes it is

CHRIS. Why do you have a loaded gun in here?

MARGARET. For when my husband's evil sister breaks out of prison!

BERNADETTE. I got a presidential pardon!

MARGARET. Not yet, you don't, and now that he's dead, you never will – UNLESS you help us come up with a plan and deal with his body.

BERNADETTE. And then what – he comes back to life and pardons me?

HARRIET. You get us through today, I will sign your pardon for him. I forge his signature all the time.

JEAN. Not on *official* documents!

HARRIET. Oh I'm sorry, is THAT the ethical line we've decided not to cross today? She's probably the only one here who knows what to do with a body, right?

(*To* **BERNADETTE.**) I bet you even got a guy just for bodies, right?

BERNADETTE. Charlie is good at what he does.

HARRIET. Exactly. You help us out, within twenty-four hours we all walk free. Tell us what to do.

　　　;

BERNADETTE. Suicide. We make it look like he killed himself.

CHRIS. Right, because people smash their skulls against marble suffragists all the time.

HARRIET. If we stage it right we could make it look like he overdosed, passed out, and hit his head on the way down.

MARGARET. Why would he commit suicide in *my* office?

BERNADETTE. Your personality, your voice, the décor...

HARRIET. She's right, we have to move him and clean up all evidence of any

STEPHANIE. Blooddddd!

(**STEPHANIE** *has dipped her hands in the puddle of blood oozing in the doorway and is joyfully smearing it on her face and body.*)

JEAN. Oh my god

STEPHANIE. Blooooooooood

HARRIET. No, Stephanie? Stephanie, look at me

STEPHANIE. Blood / paint blood paint blood paint

HARRIET. I know you feel weird right now, but you need to hold it together, okay? Stephanie, you are the presidential secretary, / remember?

STEPHANIE. I AM WOMANNNN

HARRIET. Yes, yes you are, and

STEPHANIE. SPACE! MY SPACE

(**STEPHANIE** *starts smearing blood across the walls.*)

MARGARET. No, not the wallpaper – GRAB HER

(**STEPHANIE** *zeroes in on* **MARGARET**:)

STEPHANIE. YOU! You are NOT NICE TO ME

HARRIET. Stephanie, I think this is a great opportunity to calmly express

STEPHANIE. YOU DIE NOW

(*She charges at* **MARGARET**.)

MARGARET. HELP I can't run in Crocs! I can't run in Crocs!

JEAN. How long is she gonna be like this?

BERNADETTE. I don't know, she's got the tolerance of a hamster, but she seems to be going through all the normal stages

JEAN. What are the normal stages?

BERNADETTE. Visions, belligerence, mania, unquenchable sexual thirst, and vomiting.

> (**CHRIS** *dangles keys, trying to distract* **STEPHANIE**.)

CHRIS. Look, honey, keys! Oooooh, keys!

> (**STEPHANIE** *finds the keys threatening. She growls and lunges for* **CHRIS**.)

NOPE, doesn't like keys!

BERNADETTE. I think we're pretty firmly in Belligerence.

MARGARET. The door – she's heading for the

> (**DUSTY** *reenters from the hall, hitting* **STEPHANIE** *hard in the face with the door.* **DUSTY** *vomits blue.*)

My carpet!

DUSTY. Gross, sorry, I'm normally fine with swallowing, but this pregnancy has thrown me all off.

CHRIS. You said forty-five minutes!

DUSTY. They were so excited, but it's okay, I left them asleep in the closet. They looked so cute together, you didn't tell me they were twins!

JEAN. Twins? They're / not

DUSTY. It's amazing they can protect the president even though one of them is blind and one of them is missing an arm.

JEAN. Oh my GOD, the vets – she blew the VETERANS!

DUSTY. Ohhh. You know, that makes more sense.

BERNADETTE. What a surprise that the blowjob plan backfired, that one seemed airtight.

DUSTY. Hey! We all serve in different ways and if I can provide any relief to those brave men I consider that a win!

HARRIET. Wait, what's happening, I can't hear the TV!

> *(From the TV:)*
>
> *"...president reportedly stormed out of the nuclear non-proliferation discussions, after a fiery exchange with the Prime Minister of Bahrain."*

No no no

> *"Sources within the White House say the president refused to sit for the duration of the negotiations, which the prime minister and several other world leaders interpreted as, quote, 'an aggressive power move.'"*

You FUCKER

> **(HARRIET** *lunges at the president's body. Everyone rushes to restrain her.)*
>
> *"The White House has yet to release an official statement, but the prime minister says there will be, quote, 'regretful consequences.'"*

After everything I do to get you here

JEAN. Stop it shut up / they'll hear you

HARRIET. I'm going to follow you to hell!

BERNADETTE. Get the sweater! / Gag her

MARGARET. Dusty, hit her again!

DUSTY. I don't want to hurt her, I don't know my own strength!

> **(JEAN** *slaps* **HARRIET. HARRIET** *crumples.)*

JEAN. Sorry oh my god are you okay? Harriet?

(All fight gone, limp with despair:)

HARRIET. *(Crying.)* I'm never gonna have a shot in five years, not even for vice president

DUSTY. *(Soothing.)* Hey, no, don't say / that

HARRIET. *(Crying harder.)* I thought my haircut made me look presidentiaaaaal

CHRIS. *(Encouraging.)* It *does*. You look just like Reagan.

HARRIET. *(Sobbing.)* Noooo trickle-down economics are the worrrrst

JEAN. Hey, hey, stop it, listen to me: we can still contain this.

HARRIET. It's too much

JEAN. No it's not

HARRIET. I'm too tired

JEAN. No you're not

HARRIET. Let's just go to prison, Jean, maybe it's not so bad. You could teach me how to be a lesbian

JEAN. That's not how lesbians work and no one's going to prison! This is what we're going to do: Margaret takes the endorsement. Tweak the speech to make it your own, stretch it as long as you can, look happy, look easy, look

MARGARET. Earthy.

JEAN. Sure. While she's got the press, we move the body. The vets are conked out with their cocks out, so we can cross them off the schedule – thank you, Dusty

DUSTY. They're the real heroes.

JEAN. Okay. Chris – you know how to get blood and vomit out of upholstery?

CHRIS. I do it after every playdate.

JEAN. Stay visible, don't talk to each other, go about your days. And then tonight, right when he's supposed to be onstage for his FML speech, POTUS will be found across the White House with three horse tranquilizers up his butt and a suicide note in his hand.

MARGARET. That could work.

CHRIS. It's brilliant.

BERNADETTE. *(To* **JEAN.***)* I've never been so attracted to you in my life.

JEAN. Whaddya say, Harry?

HARRIET. We got Bahrain. We got cabinet members on drugs. We got two hundred feminists coming to dinner pissed about cunty – that shit won't go away just cuz he's dead

JEAN. *But it will!* Think about it: you can't go after a guy who just killed himself. You can't criticize a country in mourning. That would be *distasteful*!

HARRIET. But

JEAN. He was unwell. He can't be held responsible for his words, or his actions, he can't be held to etiquette or facts – *he was sad!*

HARRIET. But

JEAN. This is what you *do*, Harry. You stand in for him every single day, you've done it for *years*. You clean up his messes, you make excuses, you do his job, and then you wake up and do it all over again. But what if today is different?

What if *this* is the last mess of his you ever have to clean?

What if it's All. Finally. Over.

(STEPHANIE has disentangled herself partway from her bondage and is standing in the stage-right doorway.)

STEPHANIE. Bye-bye.

2.2

(The **WOMEN** *vs. the world.)*

*(***STEPHANIE** *careens through the White House.)*

STEPHANIE. IT'S ALL MIIIIIIIIIIIIINNNNNEE

HARRIET. *(On the phone.)* What do you mean, "Why would Norway involve itself?" Because that's what allies do, Hilde. You back us and in exchange we give you things that Norway needs, like peanut butter and genetic diversity. Oh nice, Hilde, you eat your herring with that mouth?

*(***JEAN** *faces the press:)*

JEAN. Do I seem worried? No, Eric, please don't speak until I call on you. If I don't seem worried then I must not be worried – No, like I said, the talks did not stall, they just broke for lunch. Well maybe the Saudi minister wanted to go home for lunch, Eric, did you think about that? – No, I don't see your hand – Look, if POTUS were worried, then I would be worried, but we've established I'm *not* worried, so by that logic – *Hand, Eric*

> *(***MARGARET** *and* **HARRIET,** *on the move.* **MARGARET** *practices the endorsement, and* **HARRIET** *scribbles revisions to the speech while talking on the phone.)*

MARGARET. "Leslie Hopper is not only a dear friend, but a fellow activist"

HARRIET. *(Into the phone.)* Absolutely, Javier. And you can tell the ambassador that nobody

MARGARET. "Who has dedicated her life to serving"

HARRIET. *(Into the phone.)* Is undermining these negotiations, least of all

MARGARET. "That glorious state our president"

HARRIET. *(Correcting* **MARGARET.***)* My husband

MARGARET. "My husband / hails from"

HARRIET. *(Covering, into the phone.)* President!

MARGARET. *(To* **HARRIET.***)* You have the handwriting of a drunk baby!

HARRIET. *(Into the phone.)* When I say husband I mean president, because, because what is the president if not America's husband, am I right?

> *(Across the White House,* **BERNADETTE** *and* **CHRIS** *hurry down the hall, peering into rooms.* **CHRIS** *holds her dripping breasts, trying to stop them from bouncing as she runs.)*

CHRIS.	BERNADETTE.
Ow	Shut up.
ow	Shut up.
ow	Shut up.

CHRIS. She couldn't have gotten far. What's in there?

BERNADETTE. Just dudes in suits.

> **(CHRIS** *peers into a room, then jumps back from the door, grabbing* **BERNADETTE.***)*

CHRIS. *(Whispering.)* Shit! He sent Nate!

BERNADETTE. Who's Nate?

CHRIS. A snot-faced preteen who thinks he's a journalist. Dammit, I *told* Alan I had this story locked down!

BERNADETTE. You told your boss you had a big story? / Are you crazy?

CHRIS. I didn't know! That was this morning! Back when skies were still blue and grass was still green and my big scoop was cunty!

BERNADETTE. Harriet is moving dead POTUS across the White House *right now* and you have literally invited / a journalist

CHRIS. I didn't invite him! If I had it my way that preppy little WASP would be strung up by his

Nate! Hi!

Oh, were you in there? I didn't see you, how funny, I was just looking for, um, the, um

(She remembers her breastmilk stains.)

bathroom. Ha ha. Clearly having a bit of a frazzled – What? Oh, yes, sorry, this is, um

BERNADETTE. Chanterelle.

CHRIS. ...Chanterelle. My, um, my, um / babysitter.

BERNADETTE. Girlfriend.

CHRIS. Former babysitter, current girlfriend. Hey, in this post-feminist world, women can run off with the nanny too *ha ha*

STEPHANIE. Post it post it post it post it post it post it post it

> *(**STEPHANIE** is backing down the hall, sticking Post-it notes on every surface, a few notes stuck to her forehead. She sees them, freezes, tries to make a run for it. **BERNADETTE** nabs **STEPHANIE** by the inner tube and drags her, struggling, back to **CHRIS**.)*

CHRIS. *(Trying to stay breezy.)* And this is Stephanie. She's our house / keeper

BERNADETTE. Slave.

CHRIS. No!

BERNADETTE. Sex slave.

CHRIS. Consensual! Voluntary. Loves it. We all do. Anyway, Nate, I got everything handled here, so why don't you go back to the office and – pardon?

No no Alan must have misunderstood me. When I said big story I meant my profile on the First Lady. Gonna be big. The "woman behind the Botox" that sort of –

No, you don't need to, I'm saying there's nothing here.

(Losing all breeziness.) What do you *mean*, "Perhaps I'm not the best judge of that."

BERNADETTE. *(Warning.)* Babe, why don't we

CHRIS. You know what, Nate? Fuck you. Because there *is* a story. A big, fat, juicy story

BERNADETTE. Darling

CHRIS. A behemoth of a story, that I dug up, that's *mine*, that will be printed with *my* name on it, and if you try to take it from me, I will stab you in the throat with that hipster fucking fountain pen you love so much

BERNADETTE. *(Impressed.)* Oh shit

CHRIS. What do you mean, "Does Greg know about all this?" Is that supposed to be some kind of threat?

BERNADETTE. I think it is

CHRIS. Like if I don't give you my story you're gonna tell my ex-husband I'm gay now, is that it?

BERNADETTE. Get it, girl

CHRIS. You know what? Go ahead. Please do. Tell him after nine years of blowing *his* crooked little cock, I'm finally getting *mine* from my girlfriend Chanterelle and our live-in sex slave!

BERNADETTE. YAS BITCH

CHRIS. I'm getting eaten out for DAYS, motherfucker!

BERNADETTE. / For DAYS

CHRIS. MY PUSSY IS QUEEEEEEEEEN

BERNADETTE. *(Dancing up on **STEPHANIE**.)* She be / royalty, call her Your Majesty

CHRIS. *(Calling after Greg.)* Yeah you BETTER run!

*(To **BERNADETTE**.)* That was AMAZING!

BERNADETTE. FIRE! / You were on FIRE!

CHRIS. I feel so ALIVE!

BERNADETTE. You would *dominate* prison!

CHRIS. Really? You think so?

> *(**STEPHANIE** bites **BERNADETTE**, attempting to escape:)*

BERNADETTE. OW – cool it, bitch

CHRIS. *(Still amped up.)* YEAH, BITCH!

I'm so sorry, I actually really don't like calling other women / that

BERNADETTE. Wait someone's coming

CHRIS. The closet, get her in the

> *(They try to shove **STEPHANIE** into the closet. She resists. They both have to hold the door shut.)*

BERNADETTE. This looks suspicious!

CHRIS. Here, just

> *(**CHRIS** grabs **BERNADETTE** and kisses her, just as **JEAN** comes around the corner.)*

JEAN. The FUCK?

BERNADETTE. / Shit

JEAN. I'm sorry, should I *leave*?

CHRIS. Of / course not, we need your help

BERNADETTE. Babe, we were just covering, we didn't know who was coming and we needed to act like

JEAN. No, no, it's fine. I'm just surprised, Bernie, I didn't realize you preferred your pussy post-partum these days.

CHRIS. Hey!

BERNADETTE. Take it easy, Chris didn't do anything wrong.

JEAN. *Sure*, why would *anyone* take responsibility for *anything* when Jean will take responsibility for *everything*, right? / That's the way it's always been

CHRIS. What is her problem?

BERNADETTE. You really want to get into this now? Look, I know when we were hooking up / I gave you some mixed messages

CHRIS. Ohhh...

JEAN. You got stoned at my dad's funeral, asked me to marry you, and then screwed the caterer!

CHRIS. Guys guys GUYS

> (**STEPHANIE** *has slipped from the closet and is running gleefully down the hall.*)
>
> (*Meanwhile...*)
>
> (**HARRIET** *and* **DUSTY** *next to the FML box, amidst a pile of FML t-shirts. They've gotten the president into the box and mostly concealed him with t-shirts, but his feet are still visible. Both are bloody and disheveled from moving the body.*)

DUSTY. Hall's clear.

HARRIET. Wait – put this on.

> *(She tosses* **DUSTY** *a t-shirt and puts one on herself.)*

DUSTY. Oh my god these are hilarious! We gotta take a selfie. / Wait, let's get the box behind us

HARRIET. *What?* Are you crazy? Give me that phone!

DUSTY. But FML! Like, *FML*?

HARRIET. The Female Models of Leadership Council!

DUSTY. Ohhh wow I thought you were in your sixties but you're older, aren't you?

HARRIET. I'm not sixty!

DUSTY. *(Concerned.)* Really? Your skin might age better if you stop eating gluten.

HARRIET. *(Gripping her side of the box.)* And the world might be better if you stop eating the president's butthole, but we can't have everything, can we! Lift on three: One, two

> *(On the front lawn,* **MARGARET** *addresses the press:)*

MARGARET. Which is why it is with great pride and joy that the president and I endorse Leslie Hopper as the next governor of

> *(***MARGARET*** *freezes as* **STEPHANIE** *appears behind the crowd: underwear, inner tube, covered in blood and Post-it notes.)*

but but but while I have you all looking at me – your attention, eyes here, eyes front. While I have your attention, I, um, would like to take this moment to address

(**STEPHANIE** *scurries across the space and exits.* **CHRIS**, **BERNADETTE**, *and* **JEAN** *appear, breathless from pursuit, looking frantically for* **STEPHANIE**.)

MARGARET. *(Trying to signal to them which way she went.) That way –*

(Covering, back to the crowd.) That way, that singular way, that America must lead the charge in

(**STEPHANIE** *appears again. She tiptoes toward* **CHRIS**, **BERNADETTE**, *and* **JEAN**, *who are looking in the opposite direction.* **MARGARET** *tries to get their attention:)*

Turn around – turning around the, um, the search for, um – *Christ!*

(**STEPHANIE** *has tapped* **JEAN** *on the shoulder and tried to run away.* **CHRIS**, **JEAN**, *and* **BERNADETTE** *all dive on top of her in a dogpile. There's a struggle.)*

(Watching in horror.) So um, in summation. America has lost its way when it comes to our backwards – *Jesus!* – views on – *oh god* – God, Jesus and God – where is America on that subject, I ask. Lost, that's where, and and I think a good thing to do would be to take this time to – *grab her hair* – hands, grab hands, clasp hands and pray. With our eyes closed. That's good, EVERYONE CLOSE THEIR EYES.

(As **BERNADETTE**, **CHRIS**, *and* **JEAN** *drag* **STEPHANIE** *bodily off:)*

And let us pray.

(The world becomes louder, faster, angrier. Overlapping soundbites boom from the heavens with an increasingly God-like quality. The **WOMEN** *scramble to keep*

up, hurrying down halls, popping out of doors, appearing out of nowhere and then disappearing just as abruptly. Throughout the following, **HARRIET** *laboriously drags the FML box across the White House – perhaps a foot occasionally pokes out and* **HARRIET** *hurries to push it down.)*

"...a chaotic day at the White House..."

STEPHANIE. SPAAAAAAAAAAAACE

CHRIS. *(Wrangling* **STEPHANIE.***)* She's a performance artist

"...more drama at the White House..."

BERNADETTE. *(Wrangling* **STEPHANIE.***)* One of those Make-A-Wish kids

"...confusion at the White House..."

DUSTY. Are *you* Kevin or Danny?

"...guests tweeting they will not be attending..."

HARRIET. No comment.

DUSTY. *(Flirty.)* Are you *sure*?

"...president has yet to comment..."

(Still trying to be sweet.) I feel like you guys might be lying to me

"...First Lady tells nation to 'close eyes and pray'..."

JEAN. – A gross misinterpretation of her speech, which was, at its core, a

"...heavily Christian message..."

BERNADETTE. Trust me, no one is more godless than Margaret.

MARGARET. Well Jesus was Jewish

"trending with Evangelicals"

DUSTY. *(No more sweetness.)* That's it! No one's getting blown 'til I see some ID!

"Germany uncomfortable"

"Israel pulls out"

"Will the president be responding?"

"Is there a response?"

"What game is he playing?"

"Who is running this country?"

STEPHANIE. MEEEEEEEEEEEE

"ARE WE ALL GOING TO DIE?"

HARRIET. No comment.

2.3

*(**HARRIET** and **JEAN** in the bathroom with the
FML box. One of POTUS's legs is dangling
over the side of the box.)*

HARRIET. France is out!

JEAN. *Out?* What do you mean "out"?

HARRIET. They're OUT they're refusing to resume the talks
and if France is out then Britain's out and if Britain's
out then China's out and if China's / out

JEAN. But why is France out

HARRIET. Because Bahrain's out

JEAN. Because of cunty?

HARRIET. Because of Thailand!

JEAN. Thailand's pissed at Bahrain because of cunty?

HARRIET. Thailand's pissed at POTUS 'cause he was cunty
to Bahrain

JEAN. But he wasn't cunty, he just couldn't sit down because
of the thing on his

HARRIET. I KNOW, Jean, but we can't tell the world about
the thing on his

JEAN. It's better than the world thinking he was a cunt to
Bahrain

HARRIET. Everyone's a cunt to Bahrain! Nobody cares
about Bahrain!

JEAN. Except Thailand

HARRIET. Nobody cares about Thailand

JEAN. Except France

HARRIET. France doesn't care, they're just looking for an excuse to humiliate us ever since the / shit with Syria!

JEAN. Shit with Syria – goddammit, Harriet, you promised me good optics on these talks! Three of the performers I booked for tonight have canceled. The poet laureate just tweeted a haiku titled FML

HARRIET. Haikus are nice!

JEAN. This one WASN'T!

HARRIET. It's not my fault! How could I know that every country and their mother would be itching for an excuse to make us look like incapable war-mongering idiots?

JEAN. *(Losing it.)* How could you – HOW COULD YOU KNOW? POTUS has spent three years burning EVERY BRIDGE, insulting EVERY ALLY, and finger-banging EVERY DIPLOMAT'S WIFE around the world! I mean, hey, it's ALMOST as if America doesn't have an endless line of moral credit –

I mean who'd have THUNK there was a limit to how much ethical currency a country could just THROW AWAY before every other nation finally claps back, "YA BROKE, BITCH!"

> (**MARGARET** *runs in, dressed for the gala in a gown and her Crocs.*)

MARGARET. There / you are!

HARRIET. Where have you been?

MARGARET. I didn't know where you were! We said we'd meet at the Residence!

HARRIET. I texted you "With POTUS in Bathroom!"

MARGARET. You texted me "With potty in buttroom!"

JEAN. My phone is exploding right now. What am I telling the press?

HARRIET. You want to switch jobs, Jean? How about *I* come up with the soundbite and *you* can stick suppositories up the dead president's asshole

JEAN. I got *New York Times* asking if we're going to war

MARGARET. Guests are already starting to arrive for the gala. We need to get him to the Residence and those tranqs up his ass right now

HARRIET. Too many people are looking for him. Senator Kobb caught me in the hall and the only way I could get rid of him was by saying I had diarrhea – We need to do this now!

Where is Bernadette?

MARGARET. They can't find his body in the women's bathroom!

> (**HARRIET** *starts pulling POTUS's leg, but the rest of him doesn't budge.*)

HARRIET. Why not? Maybe, okay maybe he took the drugs, thinking he would have enough time before they hit to do one final speech, one final night of service – But then just before going in, he started to feel sick, ran to the nearest bathroom to throw up, hit his head on the toilet edge, and died alone in a pool of his own vomit

> (**DUSTY** *enters, carrying two garment bags.* **HARRIET** *and* **JEAN** *dive onto the body, and* **MARGARET** *pulls a gun from under her skirt.*)

/ OCCUPIED

JEAN. SHE'S POOPING

DUSTY. DON'T SHOOT I'M CARRYING THE PRESIDENT'S / BABY

HARRIET. Shhh! Shut up! Close the door!

(To **MARGARET.***) Why do you have a gun on you?*

MARGARET. I always have a gun on me.

DUSTY. Are we at war? Because Twitter feels, like, extra war-y right now.

JEAN. *(Frantically texting and tweeting, as her phone blows up.)* I'M WORKING ON IT

DUSTY. *(To* **HARRIET.***)* I got POTUS's tux, but I couldn't find your gala outfit, all I found was this weird man's suit.

HARRIET. That IS my gala outfit – it's a woman's dress tux!

MARGARET. *(Holding up the suit, disgusted.)* Christ, it's like if Elton John did Civil War reenactments.

HARRIET. You are literally wearing the footwear of a hospice worker!

MARGARET. They're EARTHY

HARRIET. I could shove those Crocs down your throat and bury your corpse in a compost heap and you STILL wouldn't be earthy!

JEAN. *(Panicked.)* Korea Korea Korea's tweeting

HARRIET. Which Korea

JEAN. The SCARY one that TWEETS

HARRIET. *(Grabbing the phone.)* Give it to me!

JEAN. It's just a stupid joke mocking POTUS for the talks falling apart. So long as nobody responds

HARRIET. Kyle just responded

MARGARET. Kyle who

HARRIET. CABINET MEMBER KYLE

JEAN. WHY WOULD KYLE TWEET AT NORTH KOREA

HARRIET. 'CAUSE HE'S HYPED ON ROIDS YOUR GIRLFRIEND SOLD HIM!

JEAN. *(On the phone.)* PICK UP YOUR PHONE, KYLE, PICK UP YOUR

DUSTY. *(Texting on her phone.)* Wait I got him!

HARRIET. How?

DUSTY. I found him on Hinge.

HARRIET. What's a Hinge?

MARGARET.   **JEAN.**
(With concern.) / Oh, girl.   *(With concern.)* Very sad.

DUSTY. Okay, he's retracting the tweet, but if you want to be extra careful I could just hack his account and freeze all his socials?

HARRIET. You *hack*?

> (**CHRIS, BERNADETTE,** *and* **STEPHANIE** *crash into the bathroom.* **STEPHANIE** *has stolen a full-sized American flag, ripped a hole in it, and is wearing it like a strange poncho.* **CHRIS** *is struggling to talk on the phone, gripping* **STEPHANIE** *with her free hand.* **HARRIET** *and* **JEAN** *dive onto the body and* **MARGARET** *draws her gun.)*

/ DIARRHEA

JEAN. WE'RE SHITTING

> (**BERNADETTE** *responds instantly to the sight of a gun, drawing her own gun and a blowtorch.)*

BERNADETTE. YOU WANNA FINISH THIS NOW, MARGE, LET'S GO

MARGARET. *(Without lowering her gun.)* Calm down, I didn't know it was you

BERNADETTE. Likely story

JEAN. *Why do you have a blowtorch?*

BERNADETTE. I always have a blowtorch.

HARRIET. Weapons down, both of you!

MARGARET. You lower, / I'll lower

BERNADETTE. *You* lower, I'll lower

HARRIET. *(Snatching their weapons from them.)* Give me that! / Now!

STEPHANIE. *(Manically, in an old-man voice.)* "When in the Course of human events it becomes / necessary for one people to dissolve the political bands…"

BERNADETTE. She's been shouting the Declaration of Independence on loop in five different languages since we pulled her out of the pastry kitchen

HARRIET. It's been *hours*, how is she STILL manic?

CHRIS. *(On the phone.)* So did he ice it?

JEAN. *(Lunging for the phone.)* No phones! Who are you talking to!

CHRIS. *(Holding the phone out of reach.)* The dance school called because your monster truck of a child *jetéd* into my kid and knocked him down!

JEAN. *(Still grappling for the phone.)* A warm breeze would knock your kid down, he's like an anemic leaf

STEPHANIE. "La vie, la liberté, et la poursuite du bonheur"

CHRIS. *(Loudly into the phone, still dodging* **JEAN.***)* I agree, Miss Belsky, aggression is learned in the home.

BERNADETTE. Didn't we smash her phone?

JEAN. *(Hanging on* **CHRIS.***)* / Give it to me!

CHRIS. *(Struggling with* **JEAN.***)* It's my backup. I got two of everything in my bag.

BERNADETTE. Why?

CHRIS. / I'M A MOM

JEAN. SHE'S A MOM

STEPHANIE. "La Vida, la Libertad, y la Búsqueda de la Felicidad"

HARRIET. ENOUGHHHHHHHHHH!

(**DUSTY** *snaps a hot selfie.*)

Really?

DUSTY. Sorry, Kyle wanted a pic.

HARRIET. I DON'T HAVE TIME FOR THIS. FML guests are already starting to arrive! We have to do this now. We have to get the tranqs in him and make it look like he hit his head on the toilet edge.

JEAN. And then what?

HARRIET. We head to the gala and stick to the plan!

JEAN. We can't just leave the body! What if something happens to it?

HARRIET. What's he going to do – stand up and walk out?

(*The president's other leg swings of its own accord over the side of the box. Everyone screams.*)

2.4

(Backstage at the FML gala. Offstage, the din of guests. **HARRIET** *is on the phone.)*

JEAN. They patched up his head, they cleaned him up, they're putting him in a tux but he's not waking up

HARRIET. *(Covering the phone.)* What do you *mean* he's not waking up? I spent three months writing this speech that he's supposed to be delivering right now.

DUSTY. I'm sure he'll be up in a sec! He seems totally fine. We propped him up in the wing on the other side of the stage. I think he's just a sweepy weepy wittle pwesident who needs a nap.

HARRIET. Oh DOES he! Is the WITTLE PWESIDENT a bit ty-ty from being an abomination to diplomacy? GODDAMMIT, I just wanted ONE NIGHT where we could feel like the President of the United States cared about OUR RIGHTS!

DUSTY. *You* should give the speech!

HARRIET. What?

*(***MARGARET*** enters.)*

MARGARET. Where is he? The feminists are getting restless.

JEAN. He's not up yet. Stall them.

DUSTY. *(To* **HARRIET.***)* You wrote the speech, you should deliver it.

JEAN. She's right, you know it better than he does.

HARRIET. But even if I did, we still need POTUS to *be* there, otherwise they'll think his absence is a statement!

DUSTY. Okay but maybe we don't need the president, maybe we just need

(**BERNADETTE** *runs in wearing a tux.*)

BERNADETTE. Yo, how sexy is this: I traded some crack with one of the waiters for his tux.

DUSTY. ...Someone who looks like him!

MARGARET. / Brilliant.

JEAN. Absolutely not.

DUSTY. We put some glasses on her, slick back her hair, from the stage no one will be able to tell!

JEAN. Of course they'll be able to tell!

BERNADETTE. I haven't been crowned Kansas City Drag King Emperor three years in a row for nothing. I got this.

DUSTY. I'll stall the crowd while you get ready!

JEAN. How are *you* going to stall the

(**DUSTY** *hands* **MARGARET** *her phone.*)

DUSTY. *(Fierce.)* BitchBeats Playlist. Karaoke version. I want the bass loud and the lights hot. Plug her in, Marge!

> *(She ties up her FML shirt into something cuter and takes the stage. Offstage, she can be heard riling up the crowd:)*

(Offstage.) **"HELLO DC! We got some angry bitches in the house TONIGHT!"**

JEAN. *(About* **BERNADETTE.***)* This isn't going to work! This woman is not capable of even pretending to be anything other than exactly what she is: / an irresponsible, selfish

MARGARET. Get changed, Harry. Wait in the other wing, Bernie. I'll signal when we're ready.

(**MARGARET** *exits.*)

DUSTY. *(Offstage.)* **Where my Iowa girls at? Who loves a big caucus?**

> (**BERNADETTE** *has whipped out some bolt cutters and goes to clip her ankle monitor.*)

JEAN. *What are you doing?*

BERNADETTE. Last I checked, POTUS doesn't have an ankle monitor.

JEAN. If you take that off before your pardon you go straight back to prison!

BERNADETTE. Yeah well, *E pubis umami*, you know?

JEAN. *E PLURIBUS UNUM*, you idiot! WAIT

> (**BERNADETTE** *cuts through the monitor.*)

(Edge of tears.) No! You can't go back there! You can't leave me again!

BERNADETTE. *(Grinning.)* I knew you missed me. I'm not going anywhere, darlin': I got a guy.

> (*They kiss.*)

DUSTY. *(Offstage.)* You chickies ready to party?

BERNADETTE. Brb, gotta save democracy.

> (*She struts out.* **JEAN** *stares breathlessly after her, utterly wooed.* **CHRIS** *enters, pulling* **STEPHANIE**, *who is still wearing the American flag and inner tube.*)

CHRIS. Harriet, I need to

HARRIET. *Not now* – Mr. Prime Minister, if you can just let the translator catch up

CHRIS. *(Holding her recorder.)* I need to talk to you

HARRIET. Chris, unless you suddenly speak *Arabic* and can negotiate Bahrain back to the table

STEPHANIE. ME

> (**STEPHANIE** *grabs the phone from* **HARRIET.**)

Hey aam tehke maa I masu'ul hala'a [Hey, you're talking to the one in charge now]

HARRIET. No no NO

STEPHANIE. *Lake habibe, bella kizib ba'a* [Listen, dude, cut the crap]

HARRIET. What is she saying?

STEPHANIE. *Kif fina nelghiya hal ossa?* [What's gonna make this go away?]

HARRIET. DO YOU KNOW WHAT SHE'S SAYING

> (**STEPHANIE** *chuckles, nodding.*)

STEPHANIE. *Yalla, bshufak* [Cool, see you soon]

> (*A triumphant* **STEPHANIE** *holds the phone out, and* **HARRIET** *snatches it from her.*)

HARRIET. Sir? ...Oh. Well good. Tell the prime minister I'm glad he feels that way...

> (*Over the opening bars of a BitchBeats song,* **STEPHANIE** *licks* **HARRIET***'s cheek.**)

STEPHANIE. You're welcome

> (*The bass drops as she takes the stage.*)

> (*Onstage: The crowd roars as* **STEPHANIE** *joins* **DUSTY** *and they launch into a riotous performance. It is aggressive and patriotic*

---

*A license to produce *POTUS* does not include a performance license for any third-party or copyrighted music. Licensees should create an original composition or use music in the public domain. For further information, please see the Music and Third-Party Materials Use Note on page iii.

in all the wrong ways: full of gyration, impressive vocal riffs, and general obscenity. They are a formidable pair – **STEPHANIE** *fully in Euphoria, swinging her inner tube around, screaming the Declaration of Independence over* **DUSTY**'s *chorus. The crowd goes wild. The song ends to thunderous applause.)*

(Offstage: **HARRIET**, *alone, watches from the wings, now dressed in her woman's tux. FML guests are chanting: "One more song! One more song!"* **DUSTY** *and* **STEPHANIE** *run offstage.)*

STEPHANIE. THEY LOVE ME

(**STEPHANIE** *runs back onstage.)*

DUSTY. We'll take our bows, and then we'll introduce you, okay?

HARRIET. Oh god.

DUSTY. Don't be nervous! This is your time!

HARRIET. I'm sorry I was harsh with you, Dusty. You are an extraordinary woman.

DUSTY. Awww, I think you're so brilliant, POTUS is making a huge mistake replacing you with Andrew.

HARRIET. ...What?

DUSTY. *(Shouting in her ear.)* Firing you! / I think it's a big mistake.

HARRIET. *Firing me?*

DUSTY. Some people were saying you're the real brains in the White House. POTUS felt like the only way to prove that's not true was to fire you.

(She runs back onstage.)

(**HARRIET** *stares after her, stunned, broken. She becomes aware of* **MARGARET**'s *gun in her hand. A murderous calm settles over her.* **JEAN** *storms in, followed by* **CHRIS**.)

JEAN. You're not running it! / We will make your life hell

CHRIS. You think I'm going to be scared off by some libel lawsuits?

JEAN. What are you gonna write, huh? That you thought you killed the president with a stone suffragist? You don't have a story

CHRIS. Oh really? How about the president who would rather risk war than admit his butt hurts? Or the boss who treats his golf clubs better than he treats his staff? OR maybe it's just the man who leads his country like he loves his women: *only when we serve him!*

JEAN. Harry! Where are you going? It's almost time.

HARRIET. He's firing me.

JEAN. What are you talking about?

HARRIET. I have to – I'll be right back.

JEAN. What are you doing?

HARRIET. Just stay here, / okay

JEAN. Harry we're so close, don't do something stupid

HARRIET. I love you, Jean. You're my best friend. / I've never had a friend like you

JEAN. Put that down. What are you thinking?

HARRIET. I have to make it end.

JEAN. NO, I'm not going to let you

HARRIET. Let go – BACK / OFF!

JEAN. I WON'T LET YOU

HARRIET. I CAN'T DO IT ANYMORE! IT HAS TO END! I HAVE TO MAKE IT END

JEAN. HARRIET

> (**HARRIET** *freezes. She looks at the gun in her hand, horrified.*)

HARRIET. *(Small, broken.)* What's happened to me?

> (**JEAN** *gently approaches. Limp,* **HARRIET** *allows her to take the gun.* **MARGARET** *and* **BERNADETTE** *enter at a run:*)

MARGARET. He's awake!

HARRIET. *(Numb and dazed.)* Fuck

JEAN. Where?

BERNADETTE. Other side of the stage, waiting to go on.

HARRIET. Fuck

> (*They cluster in the wings, peering onto the stage.*)

MARGARET. We told him he took too many pain meds, blacked out, and hit his head. Idiot totally bought it.

HARRIET. Fuck.

> (*The crowd continues to cheer and chant for* **STEPHANIE** *and* **DUSTY.** **STEPHANIE** *sprints into the wings and vomits into the FML box.*)

BERNADETTE. Heyyy look who's finally coming down from her little trip.

STEPHANIE. I feel like the air is stabbing my face.

BERNADETTE. Yeah you won't be able to eat solid foods or experience joy for about a week.

DUSTY. *(From stage.)* And now the power couple you've all been waiting for – **FLOTUS and POTUSSSSSS**!

BERNADETTE. Go get 'em, Marge

JEAN. You look amazing

> (**DUSTY** *runs off, joining the* **WOMEN** *in the wings.*)

DUSTY. *(To* **MARGARET.***)* You ready? On in three, two

MARGARET. Shit! He didn't wait for me!

> (*A man's voice, trying, unsuccessfully, to quiet the crowd. The feminists continue to scream for* **STEPHANIE** *and* **DUSTY***: "Bring them back! BRING THEM BACK!"*)

CHRIS. Go anyway! They're so amped from the show they're not even letting him talk!

JEAN. Just go out when he's done with the speech.

CHRIS. No! Push him off the fucking stage!

JEAN. Not all of us can just blow up our lives, Chris

CHRIS. LOOK at our lives! Look at Harriet!

HARRIET. Fuck

CHRIS. Look at Stephanie!

STEPHANIE. What am I wearing?

CHRIS. Look around you!

DUSTY. Who's he winking at?

MARGARET. Carol, the analyst. He's been screwing her since he was elected.

CHRIS. *(To* **JEAN.***)* See?

HARRIET. Fuck.

CHRIS. *(Raising her recording device.)* I know you got more than that to say, Harry. You know where all the skeletons are

JEAN. Leave her alone!

CHRIS. *(To* **HARRIET.***)* Go on the record and get out now before you go down with him.

JEAN. Guys like that don't go down. We're the ones who'll go down.

> *(From onstage: "Bring them back! Bring them back!")*

CHRIS. *(Pointing toward the screaming crowd.)* Listen to them! They don't want him! They want an encore! He can't last if you stop saving him

JEAN. Then someone else will! He won! Lots of people love him!

BERNADETTE. They don't love him, they're just afraid of the alternative.

STEPHANIE. What's the alternative?

JEAN, BERNADETTE, DUSTY, MARGE & CHRIS. US!

                ;

HARRIET. ...Wait, does FML mean Fuck My Life?

ALL. YES!

HARRIET. I need a cigarette.

BERNADETTE. *(Giving* **HARRIET** *a cigarette.)* He looks like shit.

MARGARET. He looks like he's gonna fall.

JEAN. *(To* **HARRIET.***)* You think he's actually gonna fall?

HARRIET. Yes.

JEAN. Should we do something

HARRIET, DUSTY & MARGARET. No.

HARRIET. *(Scared, to* **JEAN.***)* Will you stay with me?

JEAN. I'm here.

DUSTY. We all are.

BERNADETTE. He's white-knuckling that podium but the fucker's still smiling

HARRIET. 'Course he is.

He doesn't know.

> (**HARRIET** *takes a long drag on her cigarette.* **CHRIS** *raises the recording device to* **HARRIET***'s mouth:*)

CHRIS. Know what?

HARRIET. *(Grim.)* ...There's a cunty dawn coming.

> (*The* **WOMEN** *stare out from the wings: tired, united, and braced for war.*)
>
> "*BRING THEM BACK! BRING THEM BACK! BRING THEM BACK!*"

End of Play

Ingram Content Group UK Ltd.
Milton Keynes UK
UKHW020613200623
423737UK00013B/409

9 780573 709999